VATICAN VEIL

The Forbidden Agreement with China

GIULIANO ZORLONI

Paperback: 978-1-967820-70-2
eBook: 978-1-967820-71-9
Library of Congress Control Number: 2025910576

This is a work of fiction.

Ordering Information:

Prime Seven Media
518 Landmann St.
Tomah City, WI 54660

Printed in the United States of America

Giammarco and Lavinia

Table of Contents

Acapulco, a soft landing

$\mathcal{I}$n the clear sky, a Gulfstream G650 operated by Private Jet stood out against the fiery Mexican sunset.

With a cruising speed of Mach 0.85 and a range of more than 7000 miles, the G650, designed for nonstop transoceanic flights, offered passengers an exceptional in-flight experience. Every detail had been designed to ensure maximum luxury and comfort, a statement of style, comfort, and prestige.

As the plane reduced altitude and began to descend toward the airport, the five passengers on board enjoyed the last sip of wine, a fine 2010 Bordeaux, savoring the end of a long transoceanic journey. The lights in the cockpit dimmed, allowing the lights of the city below to become the focal point.

The captain warned the passengers of the imminent landing while he started the alignment procedure for the runway, the passengers fastened their seatbelts, the hostesses checked that everything was in order, the flaps extended increasing the wing surface, the landing gear began its descent movement, the engines emitted a soft noise as the speed began to decrease and a gentle pitch accompanied the final descent.

The plane touched down, the contact with the runway had been barely perceptible, a trail of light smoke had risen from the tires, a sign of a perfect landing.

Once stopped, the hostess, with a smile for the passengers, began to exclude the safety system and opened the door, the ladder extended, and the hot air of Acapulco invaded the cockpit.

While waiting for the ground staff to bring the service van closer, the passengers stood up and after having collected their luggage, they prepared to disembark.

As they stepped onto the ground, they felt the fine sand blown by the wind beneath their feet and the smell of the sea mixed with that of tropical flowers, creating an atmosphere of tranquility and well-being.

"Welcome to Acapulco General Juan Alvarez International Airport, Pearl of the Pacific," the driver of the van said as they climbed aboard. He, in an elegant uniform, was ready to assist them and accompany them to a private exit point where passport control would be simplified and away from the lines of tourists that crowded the main exit.

As they stepped out, they were greeted by the sight of palm trees swaying in the sea breeze. The lights of the city shone in the distance and promised a place that never slept.

As they drove away from the airport, they knew that their journey had just begun and that this experience was only a prelude to what was to come...

Friday 7:00am |
Ponte Sant'Angelo

That morning, Rome had woken up to a pouring rain that hammered the cobblestones. Every now and then, the sound of a car or the hurried pace of a cyclist broke the quiet, but then everything returned to silence, interrupted only by the sound of the water.

At that moment if you can immagine the city where time seemed to have stopped, was a magnificent crossroads of history, art and nature, a melancholic place that allowed anyone to immerse themselves in its eternal beauty.

Lawyer Camillo Della Rovere, with his briefcase, umbrella and determined step, crossed the almost deserted Ponte Sant'Angelo. His tailored suit, a deep midnight blue, was impeccable despite the rain and the humidity in the air; the red silk tie, decorated with the symbol of the two crossed keys, seemed to reflect his determination to close the deal for which he had been paid.

He, about to conclude an important agreement, a deal that could have marked the pinnacle of his career, moved quickly towards Via del Panico, located on the other side of the Tiber.

His career had developed entirely in Rome. He had begun as a legal consultant on complex issues of canon and civil law, representing the Holy See in various cases and then, thanks to his expertise and the relationships he had developed, he had been appointed to legal roles of the Holy See and had become a lawyer of the Roman Curia and of the Apostolic Tribunal of the Roman Rota.

Crossing the bridge, his elegant and determined figure made him seem like a character from an old novel, and his every step resounded in the silence like an echo.

As he approached his destination, his gaze was fixed on the dark waters of the Tiber, his mind was focused, every detail of the contract had been carefully studied because he knew that today's meeting was unique and there could be no mistakes.

However, he could not foresee the unexpected.

A dull shot broke the morning calm, an almost imperceptible sound that was lost among the noises of the city. A sniper, hidden in the shadows of an ancient building, had been waiting for the right moment.

The bullet, fired from an AW Sniper 338 precision rifle, of English production, in use by the military and the police forces, found its target with surgical precision, leaving Camillo's body and his midnight blue suit, now stained red, inert on the cold pavement of the bridge.

The briefcase that had fallen to the ground had opened, the documents scattered on the wet pavement. The rain mixed with the blood created small red puddles. The passers-by, few and frightened, began to retreat and then stopped to observe from afar, unable to fully understand what had happened.

The tranquility was interrupted when the police, already positioned near the bridge for the usual night surveillance, after the shooting and the escape of the tourists, immediately moved to react to this unexpected emergency situation.

The first officers climbed up and walked across the bridge towards the opposite bank while calling, via radio, for reinforcements and an ambulance.

In a few minutes, the entire area was isolated and safe.

The statues of the angels observed the scene with a sad expression, as if they were aware of the tragedy that had just occurred. The city was waking up, while the fate of Camillo Della Rovere had been fulfilled.

The passers-by, kept at a distance, watched with curiosity and fear, while the media began to crowd in, trying to capture every detail. Meanwhile, the rain continued to fall and washed away the traces but not the sense of uneasiness that permeated the air.

Despite the speed of the intervention, the murderer had managed to disappear. He had vanished into the shadows of the alleys like a ghost, leaving behind only the mystery of reasons and a disoriented city.

The deputy commissioner was calmly getting up, ready to face this gloomy day, when he received a phone call from the commissioner inviting him to go immediately to Ponte Sant'Angelo.

A murder that had just occurred had provoked an unexpected reaction from an authoritative Cardinal at the Holy See.

Arriving on the scene, he immediately received the briefcase of the murdered lawyer from the agents and, as he was preparing to speak to the emergency doctor to better understand the situation, his phone rang.

The deputy commissioner put the phone to his ear and said:

"Rizzo".

Across the line, a calm but authoritative voice spoke from the shadows of the Vatican's sacred walls.

"Good morning, Doctor Rizzo. The Police Commissioner will call you soon, but given the urgency and the sensitivity of the situation, I decided to call you in advance."

The deputy commissioner, while listening, already imagined that the day would not end with a survey, some photos and the start of a murder investigation but Even it would have implications and repercussions that he was unable to determine at the time and that would go far beyond Roman jurisdiction.

After a brief pause, the Vatican voice has been continued:

"We have already asked and asking you, please, to treat the murder of the lawyer Della Rovere with the utmost confidentiality. The lawyer was operating under our direct mandate in a matter of delicate importance. We trust in your discretion and professionalism to manage the situation without alarming public opinion."

The deputy commissioner listened and his face began to stiffen with tension. "Your Eminence, I understand your request," then he nodded even though the interlocutor could not see him, "you can count on us. We will take all necessary measures to ensure that the investigation proceeds away from prying eyes."

After hanging up, he turned to his men: "Keep the area well sealed and limit the information to the bare minimum, this case is very delicate and goes beyond the usual street crime".

In the quiet of the morning, a signal from a satellite phone connected Rome to London. The connection was clear and stable, despite the terrible weather conditions above Rome at that moment.

A voice marked by the unmistakable East Sussex accent answered, breaking the silence: "Delaware". The surname was pronounced with an icy calm, as if it were a well-known code between the two interlocutors.

From Rome, the response was concise and full of meaning: "Target eliminated, Sir". He said.

The hitman's voice was firm, without a trace of emotion, without an inflection, as if the action he had just carried out was a habit, a routine.

From London, with a tone of contained satisfaction:

"Good, I'm about to send you the dossier with all the information on the professor. Stay hidden and do not act until I confirm the action."

The sentence was accompanied by the sound of keys being typed on a keyboard, a sign that the dossier had been sent in real time. The professor was obviously the next target, and the dossier contained all the crucial details for the next mission. The interlocutor checked the device and confirmed receipt of the dossier. The information was precise: photos, schedules, habits, weak points. Every detail had been collected and organized with great care.

The communication ended with a brief exchange of confirmations, and calm reigned again.

9:00am |
L'Informazione

Alessandro Conti was an investigative journalist known for his tenacity in following the darkest trails and his unerring instinct for uncovering news. His reputation often preceded him and many colleagues considered him one of the best in his field.

He had been working for *L'Informazione*, a widely followed independent Italian newspaper, for several years. Over time, the newspaper's director had given him his own editorial space, and he had repaid him by bringing the results of some of his exclusive investigations to the front page.

When news of the murder of a man on Ponte Sant'Angelo reached his desk, instinct told him that there was much more to it than met the eye and he decided to go in person to see what had happened and gather testimonies.

Upon arrival, he found the area around the bridge surrounded and blocked by the police, who were committed to maintaining the utmost secrecy about the incident.

After a quick glance, he immediately tried to find a way around the barriers. He hid under a black raincoat, similar to those worn by the police, and after a second glance, to make sure he was not being observed by the police, he took a determined step down a side alley that passed through the gardens of the French-speaking pastoral center; the city in that area was full of small alleys, made almost invisible by the pouring rain and the darkness.

From there, eluding the surveillance, he managed to find a secondary passage that took him back to Piazza di Ponte Sant'Angelo, inside the confined area near the entrance to the bridge.

After a further check, he climbed up and began to advance on the bridge, his eyes falling on the signs of a silhouette drawn on the ground with chalk. The silhouette depicted a man and, next to it, some numbered references served as indicators for the photographers of the forensic police.

Alessandro stopped for a moment to observe every detail: the body had already been removed, but the crime scene still spoke. The hitman must have shot from above and from a relatively short distance; the marks left by the exiting bullet were still, despite the rain, clearly visible on the cobblestones.

It wasn't the first time he had faced complex cases and he knew that the road to the truth would be, once again, long.

He looked back, closed his eyes and imagined a possible trajectory of the bullet, trying to trace the shooting position in his mind. Then he opened them again, aware of the importance of every small clue, he began a silent search for some further detail that could escape less attentive eyes. His experience had taught him that it was often the most insignificant details that revealed the greatest truths.

A name, an object, anything that could give a face to the victim or a motive for the murder.

He approached a police car parked on the bridge to protect the evidence from the rain and recognized the man on the identity document found by the officers. The photo was of the lawyer Camillo Della Rovere, a familiar face and an acquaintance with whom Alessandro had shared many passionate discussions in the past.

Della Rovere was a man of great knowledge, an expert in the intricate issues that concerned the Holy See and a profound connoisseur of the stories and secrets hidden beyond the Vatican walls.

A brilliant mind and analytical skills had made him a figure both respected and feared at the same time. The journalist felt a lump in his throat; every conversation, every debate they had shared now seemed like a distant echo, a precious memory to be treasured.

Now, more than ever, he felt the need to discover the truth. Not only for justice but also to honor the memory of a man who had dedicated his life to understanding a world hidden from the eyes of many.

With a heavy heart but a clear mind, he prepared to follow every lead, question every witness, and leave no stone unturned.

The truth had to emerge, and he would be there to tell it.

Monday 10:00am | Sapienza University

*H*e walked along the wide tree-lined avenue, each step accompanied by a soft crackling of leaves underfoot. The heavy rains of the previous days had refreshed and cleaned the air, his feeling was clean, serene, a beautiful feeling.

In front of him stood the imposing facade of Sapienza University. This majestic building had transformed over time into a neighborhood, a collection of buildings that seemed to enclose within their walls the wisdom of many centuries. The windows, similar to attentive eyes, reflected the movement of the clouds, the long avenues gave a sense of isolation from the noise of the city.

Like every morning, Luca crossed the entrance to the Institute of Engineering, where the ancient sculptures told stories of illustrious academics and revolutionary discoveries.

Inside, the corridors were a labyrinth of knowledge, with doors that opened onto classrooms where the curious minds of future engineers immersed themselves in passionate discussions. His footsteps echoed on the floor and mingled with the sounds of pens writing and book pages turning.

Luca stopped in front of a noticeboard covered with academic notices and posters of upcoming events, reflecting on how much his life had changed since he had crossed that threshold for the first time.

With a melancholic smile, he continued his walk inside towards the Department of Artificial Intelligence, the beating heart of the university, where another afternoon immersed in work awaited him.

A promising young engineer, he stood out for his clear and lively eyes that expressed an intelligence always in ferment, ready to decipher enigmas and accept new challenges.

Born and raised among the shady streets and stately villas of Parioli in Rome, Luca had always breathed an atmosphere of elegance and prestige. The clean streets, the well-kept parks and the chic cafes of the neighborhood had been the backdrop to his childhood and adolescence, had influenced his way of being and presenting himself to the world.

Educated in the most renowned private schools, he had developed a refined taste and a certain ease in moving among the upper social circles.

Despite the privileged environment in which he was born, in line with his generation he preferred comfortable but elegant clothing: well-ironed linen shirts, quality jeans and soft leather shoes that accompanied him on the long university days.

On his wrist, an Omega Seamaster - a gift from his father for his eighteenth birthday - a symbol of a strong family bond and a recognition of his ambitions.

Despite the pressure of exams and deadlines, he had always been accustomed to maintaining a calm attitude and a determination that had led him to be a natural leader among his colleagues.

Animated by an innate innovative spirit, he had developed a deep passion for Artificial Intelligence algorithms, a passion that had ignited over five years earlier.

This genuine interest had pushed him to explore the less traveled paths, away from passing fads and the ephemeral hype that often surrounded new technologies.

In particular, he was fascinated by the ability of Artificial Intelligence to transform data into knowledge, to learn and adapt autonomously. For him, Artificial Intelligence, called AI for Artificial Intelligence, was not just a field of study; it was a window into a future in which technology could improve people's lives.

He spent hours programming, testing, and optimizing algorithms, always looking for new methods to make machines more intelligent and intuitive.

His desk was often covered with books and articles on the latest research in the field of AI, it was not uncommon to find him immersed in animated discussions with his colleagues on new solutions or emerging methodologies.

The door of the Artificial Intelligence department opened, the young man crossed the threshold with a confident step and began to move between the workbenches where students and researchers, absorbed in their projects, seemed not to see what was happening around them.

It was there that he, along with a group of students who had become friends over time, was creating an advanced AI system, a system they had named Sherlock in honor of their professor and Sherlock Holmes.

This system used a combination of genetic algorithms and machine learning techniques to analyze large amounts of data in search of patterns and recurring models that could be used as a key to deciphering codes or ciphered texts.

Genetic algorithms were inspired by natural evolutionary processes to optimize the search for solutions, while machine learning allowed Sherlock to learn and improve its performance over time.

The combination of these technologies allowed Sherlock to tackle complex decoding tasks, simulating a "thought" process similar to the human one, but with the speed and efficiency of a computer.

Arriving at his desk, he connected to the university network and began his daily coding work; by now he and the boys were close to releasing the first version of their algorithms and the approach of this moment generated a sense of euphoria in Luca.

As the hours passed, he remained immersed in his work, the concentration was palpable, he was creating something more than just software: he was forging a tool that could change the world of coding and decoding, a tool to illuminate the dark corridors of texts and encrypted codes.

The ticking of the clock on the wall marked the passing of time and reminded him that the early afternoon was about to bring with it an important appointment.

Professor Martini, the one who had seen Luca's potential early and had guided his passion for AI, was waiting for him in his office to discuss the latest developments of Sherlock.

Luca thought back to all the times the professor had spent hours of his time helping him overcome technical obstacles, refining algorithms, seeking that perfection that only an expert mind like Martini could intuit.

Their relationship was more than a simple academic exchange, it was a bond of mutual respect and shared aspirations, so much so that Luca had accepted without question the professor's suggestion to name his intelligent automaton Sherlock.

As he prepared for this meeting, he felt a mixture of gratitude and determination, knowing that the professor would be ready to question every aspect of Sherlock to make sure it lived up to expectations.

But he was equally ready to prove that his work was not just a final-year student's dream, but a reality capable of leaving its mark on the world of coding and decoding through AI.

11:00am |
Sapienza University

The news fell on him like a sudden and unexpected weight: his mentor had just been found lifeless, poisoned, in his office, a place that had always been a hotbed of brilliant ideas and lively discussions.

An emblematic figure in the academic panorama of Artificial Intelligence, with a degree in Mathematics and a curriculum that included teachings in the most prestigious European and American universities, his name was synonymous with excellence and innovation.

Born in Monza, a city permeated by a passion for motoring, the young Martini had spent his childhood among sketches of cars and complex mathematical models of aerodynamics. This early inclination for precision and for the beauty of shapes that defy the wind had preluded his future interest in AI, a field where mathematics merged with technology to create something revolutionary.

A fanatic of Sherlock Holmes stories, he had always appreciated the famous detective's stringent logic and deductive acumen, qualities that he had transferred to his approach to scientific research. His analytical mind, combined with an innate curiosity, had led him to explore the depths of AI, and he had become a pillar of his department at Sapienza University.

With a reputation as a demanding but fair mentor, Martini was known for pushing his students beyond the boundaries of the known, to encourage them to seek innovative solutions and never settle for easy answers. His classroom was a melting pot of ideas, where complex theories came to life and where the future of AI was shaped every day.

As he approached his office, Luca felt the world slowing down around him, the sounds were muffled, he felt isolated, the corridor seemed to get longer, every step resonated with a piercing echo, he felt the oxygen becoming rarefied as if at high altitude.

The door, always wide open to welcome anyone seeking knowledge or advice, was now about to close. A newly arrived policeman had begun to lay out a yellow and black ribbon to mark the border: a reminder of how reality could be both fragile and unexpected.

Luca, who had entered just in time, began to observe. Inside, the office was a picture of interrupted quiet. Documents scattered on the desk, a book half open, the soft light of the lamp that still shone, as if refusing to acknowledge that its owner would never return to turn it off.

The air was still, full of unanswered questions, the professor was there, sitting at his desk, still too. A cup of coffee was still positioned next to a pile of documents. Everything seemed normal, except the oppressive quiet and the unnatural position of the body.

Luca immediately noticed the paleness of the professor's face and the cyanotic lips, unmistakable signs of poisoning. The professor, with his eyes closed, seemed almost at peace, but the truth was written on his face: the end had come suddenly.

On the table, next to the cup, lay a sheet of paper with a chemical formula scribbled in pencil: $C_{17}H_{19}NO_3$. The molecule of morphine. Next to it: a syringe and a series of calculations and notes, as if wanting to leave a final piece of advice.

Luca noticed something unusual, something he had never seen on the desk despite the long time he had spent with the professor in his office: an old, yellowed photograph of the professor at a young age, together with another individual he was unable to recognize. On the back, a date and a single handwritten note by the professor.

Nemesis, Stanford 1986.

The sight of the photograph triggered a memory in Luca: Nemesis was the name of a research project the professor had worked on many years before, a project shrouded in secrecy that had ceased to exist without explanation.

The trembling voice of Francesca, the professor's assistant, interrupted his flow of thoughts: "He was killed," the woman said with words that seemed like boulders.

The professor's death had not been a tragic accident, but the result of a deliberate act. The department, once a symbol of progress and innovation, had just turned into a place of crime.

The glances of those who had rushed to the rescue, at the news, met full of suspicion and fear. Who could have committed such a brutal act and why Martini, loved and respected by all?

While the investigators moved frantically along the corridors, between closed doors and delimited areas, the news deeply shook the entire academic community. Minds accustomed to solving scientific enigmas now found themselves faced with the most disturbing of mysteries.

The memory of many quickly ran to another murder that occurred on May 9, 1997 when, inside the university city, a gunshot, fired for reasons still shrouded in mystery, had hit Marta Russo, who died five days later in hospital.

The case was at the center of a complex judicial process, the enigmatic circumstances and the investigative difficulties failed to outline a clear motive, the investigations were the subject of great media coverage and public debate.

The murder of Marta Russo had since become a symbol of how fragile life could be and how, at times, the truth could escape even the sharpest minds.

The news of the imminent announcement had slipped through the shadows of the crime, but now it took on a new, sinister relevance. Martini was about to reveal to the world the creation of a complex series of algorithms that would make up a single AI technology; the professor had wanted to give this series a name that he intended to reveal with a forthcoming public announcement.

His technology was capable of correlating historical facts with a precision never seen before, a key to deciphering truths buried by time. His work promised to be a revolution in the field of historical research, a bridge between the past and the present that could rewrite entire history books.

His algorithms, the result of years of study and experimentation, were capable of analyzing and connecting events, revealing patterns and connections that had remained invisible to human eyes. With this solution, the professor could not only shed light on dark pages of history, but also challenge established narratives and thus question what everyone thought they knew.

His death now no longer seemed a coincidence, but a piece of a much larger and more complex puzzle. What hidden truths were so powerful as to justify a murder?

The Artificial Intelligence department, once a place of pure research, had become the stage for a hunt for the truth that could shake the very foundations of historical understanding.

1:00pm |
Sapienza University

"Good morning," greeted a police officer who had just entered, "I am Flavia Franco, Lieutenant from the Police Department. I was sent here with my team to carry out the first surveys. Can you give me your version of the facts and what happened?".

Francesca, in a very weak voice, replied: "Good morning, Lieutenant, it's... it's terrible, this morning we found the professor here in his office, he wasn't breathing anymore. We tried to revive him but nothing. We didn't touch anything in his office, we called you and then the Dean of the Faculty."

"Well... did the professor have enemies or situations that could have been critical?" said the Lieutenant, staring at Francesca.

"Not that I know of. He was an esteemed man, a genius in his field. He was working on an important project, something that could have changed the world of investigative journalism, or at least that's what he told me."

"Do you have any idea where we can find his notes and his computer?".

Francesca moved towards the desk while whispering: "Everything should be here in his office".

Then she stopped and pointed to a bookcase: "That drawer, the professor always kept it locked, it was his little hiding place", and pointed out that it was now inexplicably open.

The Lieutenant approached the drawer. "This could be an important detail; thank you for pointing it out to me. We will take some measurements to collect any fingerprints".

Francesca, still surprised, continued: "Only the professor knew what was in there, maybe he was looking for something, or maybe someone else was looking for something. Could it have been a robbery?".

"Certainly, but at this moment we cannot jump to any hasty conclusions. Now, if you excuse me, I have to make sure that the crime scene remains intact until the forensic team arrives".

The Lieutenant's tone was professional, and his movements were careful.

Meanwhile, amid the comings and goings of the policemen and the rustling of the forensic suits, an individual was moving with a calm that bordered on the disturbing.

A man tall, dressed in an elegant dark suit that seemed to swallow the light around him, was advancing with measured, almost choreographic steps. He had a confident bearing that made him seem at ease in that theater of momentary chaos.

His face was obscured by a baseball cap decorated with a small flag composed of two horizontal red and blue lines. Under sunglasses, he was scanning the environment carefully without revealing his intentions.

All that could be glimpsed was a square jaw and a thin scar that crossed his left cheek, an indelible reminder of a past that only he knew. He didn't speak to anyone, but he observed and listened; his presence was like a punctuation mark in a sentence that was still incomplete.

As the young Lieutenant approached to question him, the man turned, and his calm gaze met hers. There was no anxiety, just a silent wait, as if he had foreseen this moment long before it happened.

"Good morning, Lieutenant," he said in a low, controlled tone, "allow me, I am Agent Moro, of the Vatican Gendarmerie. I must inform you that the professor's death is not an isolated case. There is a parallel investigation underway, conducted by our offices in collaboration with your intelligence service AISI."

Francesco Moro, with his imposing stature and penetrating gaze, was the embodiment of integrity and dedication.

Born in the heart of the Canton of Ticino in Switzerland, he had inherited the tenacity and strength of spirit typical of Italian families who had migrated to the region. He had spent his childhood among the majestic peaks of the Engadine and had grown up with a character as solid as the mountains that had protected him.

Growing up in the crisp Alpine air and his grandparents' stories of courage, he developed an early sense of justice and a protective attitude toward others. These values drove him to join the Swiss Army, where he honed his strategic and physical skills. He became a respected soldier and a natural leader.

Before coming to Rome, Francis served as head of security at the World Economic Forum in Davos, where he demonstrated his ability to handle high-risk situations with calm and precision. His international experience and security expertise made him an ideal candidate for the Vatican Gendarmerie, where he now served with honor, guarding one of the beating hearts of Christianity.

"A parallel investigation? I wasn't aware of it," the Lieutenant said with a mixture of surprise and suspicion, "but may I ask you what nature these investigations are?".

Moro looked around before continuing: "The professor has developed a series of algorithms whose application could go well beyond the academic field. I can't reveal more to you without being authorized, but it is essential that we collaborate."

"I understand, I will be sure to talk to my superiors about it, but in the meantime I intend to proceed with the initial findings and wait for the intervention of the forensic team," said the Lieutenant while trying not to be intimidated by this cumbersome presence.

Moro almost interrupted her as he moved right in front of her until he obscured her view: "Of course, for now I would ask you to keep this conversation as confidential as possible and, if possible, I would ask you for access to all the professor's data and research. They could contain fundamental clues for our joint investigation."

The Lieutenant felt a cold shiver run down her back but immediately resumed the discussion: "I will do my best to assist you, even if my job is to search and find who committed this murder regardless of the implications".

Moro smiled, almost as if he wanted to ease the concern that had arisen: "It was a real pleasure meeting you, I hope you can make progress quickly. Please, if you discover something important, this is my phone number".

Meanwhile, Luca, his mind still clouded by the facts, reflected that triviality had never been a prerogative of his character and that perhaps, now, the time had come to act. He had to discover the perpetrator and the motive behind this inexplicable murder.

In recent months, Luca had gathered around him a group of highly prepared students. These young people, selected for their skills and their dedication to study and work, had become his most trusted collaborators in the "Sherlock" project. Aware of the importance of the project, everyone was always ready to answer any call.

Luca took his cell phone and typed a concise but meaningful message: "Guys, we are in DEFCON 1!".

DEFCON 1 was the highest alert level of the United States armed forces. This state indicated that a nuclear war was imminent or already underway. Luca had borrowed this expression from American films and in particular from an old 1981 film called "War Game". For them, this expression could not be used "lightly" but was an emergency code, a signal that indicated the request for attention and the need to organize an immediate meeting.

To the message that left no room for doubt about the seriousness of the situation, Luca added a second: "We have to meet this evening at the usual place in Piazza

Bologna, our professor Martini has been killed! I need to talk to you".

After finishing, Luca was assailed by two contrasting feelings: the first of determination, the second of despair and anguish for what had happened to his beloved professor.

Outside the room, in a secluded position, Alessandro Conti observed every person who entered and exited the professor's office. He had rushed to Sapienza University as soon as the news reached the editorial office, convinced that the close deaths of his friend Camillo and that of Professor Martini could not be a simple coincidence. His intent was to pick up some signal that could help him understand the events.

During his investigations into the lawyer's murder, he had managed to access and read some notes written inside a diary. These notes referred to Martini and one of his students, a girl Camillo seemed to care a lot about, perhaps a niece. Unfortunately, these notes had not given him any additional contribution other than to strengthen the suspicion that the two murders, which had occurred a few days apart, were connected. For this reason, he had decided to go to the university and also investigate the professor's sudden death.

His relationships with some police officers, moreover, had always allowed him to obtain information that would otherwise have been denied to him. One of these concerned precisely the murder case of his friend Camillo. Someone very important, within the Vatican walls, had asked the police to draw an informative veil on the murder. The information received now took on greater value because Francesco Moro had just entered the room.

What connections were there between the two murders?

Why had the Vatican Gendarmerie intervened in Sapienza University?

Looking around, he saw a shocked boy coming out of the room and heading towards the exit of the department. Alessandro, without any particular reason but just following his natural tendency to obey his instinct, jumped up, put on a jacket and started following him without being noticed.

8:00pm |
Piazza Bologna

When evening fell, Piazza Bologna transformed into a lively crossroads of city life. The soft lights of the street lamps came on and cast a glow on the facades of the rationalist buildings that surrounded it, while the voices of passers-by mingled with the noise of the traffic that faded as the night progressed.

University students and young locals gathered in bars and cafés, where the atmosphere was always effervescent with laughter and conversations that dispersed in the air. Families and groups of friends stopped for an aperitif or an ice cream, taking advantage of the pedestrian area in the center of the square where you could find a moment of relaxation on the benches surrounded by greenery.

On the corner with Via Livorno was the Cardini bar, a place where the young people would soon meet. The place had an old-fashioned character, with wooden walls and vintage mirrors, a 1970s decor that would have shone in another area of Rome, like San Lorenzo, but that there was in complete discord with the neighborhood and the people who frequented it.

Despite this slightly retro appearance, the owners had adopted a super-fast fiber network and all the tables in the bar had been wired with free power outlets for charging phones and laptops; these technological details had immediately attracted the so-called "techno-students", to the point of transforming it into a sort of cathedral for the students of the Faculty of Engineering.

Here, between a coffee, a quick lunch and a lively discussion, ideas were born and the foundations for innovative start-ups were laid. It was, in fact, the favorite meeting place for young talents who challenged each other in the design and creation of new algorithms, sometimes transforming their visions into entrepreneurial realities.

Often the discussions were so "deep tech" that it would have been difficult for a simple passer-by to even understand what language the kids were speaking.

At the back of the bar, in a separate room, with his eyes fixed on the entrance door, Luca was waiting for his companions to arrive while trying to calm the labored breathing that had come on from all the running he had done.

In the meantime, a solitary man had entered the bar immediately after him. He had sat down with his back against the wall and ordered a Long Island Iced Tea. A careful look would have immediately realized that the man was not there by chance: he had followed Luca since he left the university and had chosen a well-studied position, strategic to keep his back safe.

While he sipped the aperitif, his gaze hidden behind the pages of a newspaper, he observed the comings and goings of the customers without ever losing sight of Luca.

The first to arrive was Sofia.

A graduate in Engineering, she had undertaken a PhD in Artificial Intelligence at Sapienza University. She walked with a decisive step, her eyes shone with an insatiable curiosity, a reflection of a mind always active in search of new challenges. With a cup of coffee in one hand and a laptop covered in stickers in the other, Sofia was a living embodiment of technological innovation.

Her days were a continuous intertwining of codes, data and algorithms; She could talk about neural networks, decision trees, clustering, and machine learning as easily as others would discuss the climate. She was a natural leader, leading study groups and workshops, and sharing her passion and knowledge with students and graduate students.

She didn't just study theories, she put them into practice: she experimented and built predictive models that could one day transform entire industries.

Her deep understanding of the ethical implications of AI engaged her in discussions about how to ensure that machine learning was used for the common good. She was the kind of girl who didn't just follow technological progress, she tried to lead it.

Marco was next.

He walked with an aura of mystery that enveloped him like an invisible cloak. His days as a lone hacker, navigating the gray areas of illegality, were behind him, but they had left an indelible imprint on the way he thought and acted.

Now, as a cybersecurity student, he used his skills to defend rather than attack, to protect rather than expose. His eyes, once accustomed to the dim light of long nights spent in front of the screen, now shone in the light of day as he identified vulnerabilities and deciphered complex codes.

His fingers, fast and precise, seemed to dance on the keyboard with the same mastery as when he challenged the most secure systems, but now he did it to strengthen the barriers against those who still walked the path he had abandoned.

He didn't talk much about his past, but those who knew him knew that behind his facade of a model student hid an adventurous past, a time when every click could be his last.

He had learned the rules only to be able to explain them better and he could teach others how to recognize the signs of an impending attack. Despite his change of direction, Marco retained a certain rebellious charm, an attitude that dared anyone to test his defenses.

His experience of the "dark side" gave him a unique perspective, an ability to anticipate the moves of his opponents because they had once been his moves.

During his last year of high school and his first years of university, Marco had lived in Trastevere in a building occupied by hackers and gamers, an environment, at times, dark like a bat cave, with computers, chips and cigarettes everywhere.

That refuge for technology and game enthusiasts had then evolved, with the changing trends and technological evolution, into a primordial coworking and had become, after Covid, a structured workplace open to young people and companies.

The experience had shaped Marco, immersing him in a world of creativity and collaboration. He had developed technical and social skills that made him enterprising, resilient, and ready to seize any opportunity.

Finally, the last to arrive was Valentina.

Initially pushed into the group because of a crush on Luca, she quickly proved to be much more than just a psychology student attracted to a brilliant boy.

She moved with an energy that attracted glances and curiosity. Her beauty was disarming, but it was her intellectual acumen that defined her. With her flowing hair framing a focused and analytical face, Valentina embodied the fusion of aesthetics and intelligence.

Forensic psychology was not just her field of study, it was her passion. Valentina was fascinated by the intersection of the human mind and the law and dedicated herself to studying the darkest depths of the human soul.

Her pursuit of professional adventure was not driven by thrills, but by a genuine desire to make a difference, to shed light on the shadows of justice.

Her days were a succession of lectures, case studies, and internships, where she tested her theories and honed her analytical and interviewing skills. Valentina was always looking for opportunities to apply her knowledge, whether it was collaborating with law enforcement or participating in innovative research.

Despite her seriousness in her field, she brought with her a sense of adventure, always ready to dive into new experiences, to travel, to learn, and to expand the boundaries of her expertise. Her beauty was attractive, but it was her determination and thirst for knowledge that left a lasting impression.

When they arrived, even before greeting them, Luca began: "I saw him, guys. He was there, motionless, with his head thrown over the back of the chair. The position was unnatural, I think they killed him."

Then, unable to hold back the tears, he added: "Everyone loved him, we owe him something too, that's why I called you".

Their faces were shocked. The death of their beloved professor had shaken each of them, wiping out the usual atmosphere of jokes and lightheartedness. They all sat around the round table and Luca, without further preamble, took a deep breath and began to explain his plan.

"We have to find out how far he had come with the development of his algorithms, only then will we perhaps understand... the real reason for his murder".

After a few moments of silence, almost a sign of respect, interrupted only by the light clinking of cups and glasses around them, Marco, in a decisive tone, intervened: "The university data center contains all his work. If we can access it, perhaps we will find the answers we are looking for".

The idea was clear, but the implications were obvious to everyone. Accessing the data center without an authorized account was a risky operation, with possible legal consequences. However, Luca knew that only Marco, with Sherlock's help, would be able to do it.

"Marco hit the nail on the head," Sofia confirmed, turning to Luca, "I still remember the professor's lesson on vulnerability and the practical examples he gave us."

Everyone knew it wouldn't be easy. The idea of delving into the heart of the university's IT security was as ambitious as it was dangerous.

"Okay, but we have to move carefully, today I noticed several strangers in the corridors of Sapienza University," Luca said.

"I've already thought about it. We'll use the private network of the student house, that network is connected to the university and there are hundreds of active connections every day," Marco intervened as he looked around as if to see if anyone was listening to their words.

In fact, immersed in their lively conversation, they hadn't noticed the attentive gaze that was watching them from afar. The man who came in after Luca was still sitting apart and followed every gesture and every word with glacial calm. He had the skill of someone who had made observation an art: invisible in the chaos of the bar, as if he were part of the furniture, yet perfectly aware of what was happening around the kids.

At Marco's words, Luca, aware that every minute would be crucial, stood up, headed towards the cash register, paid the bill and gave the signal for the kids to follow him. It was time to put Marco's proposal to good use. The other kids, at the signal, stood up and left.

Immediately afterward, the man who was watching them also stood up, paid for his aperitif and headed towards the exit, following them.

Alessandro Conti, after following Luca through several streets of the city, had also entered the place trying to go unnoticed. He had sat down near the large window, ordered a coffee, plugged his phone in and began, with a relaxed attitude, to observe the entire room.

Every now and then he tried to listen, even though the din of the bar prevented him from understanding, to what the boys were saying or to observe if there was anything suspicious in their behavior.

At a certain point, for no specific reason, he felt he was being watched. He turned and his eyes met for an instant those of a man sitting on the other side of the place. The stranger, dressed in sportswear, seemed immersed in his thoughts, but that fleeting glance was enough to send a shiver down Alessandro's spine.

There was something strange about that man. An indefinable sensation, as if he had already met him, even though he was sure he didn't know him. He couldn't explain the reason for that discomfort, but he didn't have time to dwell on the matter: the boys had gotten up to leave.

Alessandro followed them with his gaze as they headed towards the exit. Before getting up, however, he had time to notice that the unknown individual had also gotten up and done the same thing, leaving the bar as well.

This sequence gave him the impression that the individual was following the boys and didn't want to lose sight of them. He decided not to stay and watch. He got up, paid the bill and also left the place, determined to follow both the boys and the stranger.

11:00pm |
Domus Academy

The Domus Academy student residence stood on Viale Regina Elena, a few steps from the historic Roman university and, given the size of the city, not far from Piazza Bologna. The main entrance, decorated with a marble mosaic depicting Minerva,it was a tribute to wisdom, while the walls adorned with portraits of illustrious academics gave the place an austere and solemn air.

The structure, divided into single and double rooms, had been for generations a refuge for students looking for a safe space to rest, study or, sometimes, engage in activities that were on the edge of the rules.

On the ground floor, the Convivium Academicum canteen served as the beating heart of the student community: a place to share not only meals, but also ideas, experiences and dreams. Between one bite and another, bonds were created, projects were discussed and academic and personal challenges were faced, a sort of microcosm of university life, where collaboration and comparison were the order of the day.

It was in this very place that Marco had met Sofia, some time before, and through her he had then come to know Luca.

The complex also housed a gym open day and night, perfectly equipped for all sports needs, and a small multifunctional auditorium, intended for conferences, screenings, shows and concerts.

That afternoon, however, Luca and Marco were not interested in the conviviality of the canteen or recreational activities.

As soon as they arrived, they had immediately secluded themselves in a corner of the internal garden, a natural place and meeting point, where the beauty of nature merged with academic life.

Shortly after, Sofia and Valentina joined them, each with her own laptop, they arranged themselves in a circle, ready to operate at Marco's commands.

Marco, sitting in semi-darkness, was visible only by the reflection of the Mac's light on his face. In silence, he was preparing to establish a connection with the university.

The first step, like in a spy game, was a meticulous scan of the network in search of open ports and vulnerabilities in the firewalls, invisible guardians that protected the IT infrastructure of the Artificial Intelligence department.

Marco knew that even the slightest mistake would set off alarms on the surveillance monitors, but adrenaline pushed him to continue without fear. After all, he had found himself in this situation hundreds of times in the past or in even more complicated situations, and today he even lived their absence with a sense of unease.

In reality, he could have used his official student credentials but, given the attention that was being concentrated around the professor and this murder, it was preferable to find an alternative and silent connection, almost imperceptible, like a shadow, to move without being identifiable.

After half an hour of trying, when the stress and tiredness were starting to take their toll, the screen lit up: the university logo appeared. "We're there," Luca muttered with a nervous smile, while raising his fist upwards.

Marco nodded without taking his eyes off the monitor. "We're in, but finding access to the server will be a whole other story."

The boys' enthusiasm was immediately dampened by a new level of security: Martini, who feared external actions more than anything else, had set up an additional level of security and defense independent of that of the university.

Marco realized this and, while on the one hand he understood the reason, on the other he was aware that this meant starting almost from the beginning.

This challenge excited him, he considered it a sort of chess game against the professor or at least against his cyber security skills.

Marco set off again and, with skill and precision, began to overcome, one after the other, all the obstacles until he found himself in front of the last bastion: the final authentication.

Sitting in front of the computer with his eyes fixed on the screen, breathing slowly, his jaw clenched, he looked at his decoding program and started it.

The program was based on an algorithm developed together with an unknown hacker he had met years before. Both had worked together on this algorithm without ever meeting in person. The result of this effort was now decoding an access code, the job for which it had been designed.

Marco, without getting distracted and keeping all his attention on the objective, ventured: "If my algorithm works, we should be able to find an access password in a few minutes".

After a few moments of nervous waiting, the algorithm emitted a beep and a message appeared on the screen: "Password successfully decoded".

"We did it," Luca rejoiced, watching Marco from over his shoulder, "now we have full access to the server."

Marco, unable to contain his enthusiasm, entered the last string of code and pressed enter. The server activated and numerous folders appeared on the screen containing the works that the professor had supervised during all his academic years.

However, the attention of the boys immediately focused on one folder in particular, with an unmistakable name: "Cognitive Optimization Algorithms - Prof. Martini".

The AI was there. Marco double-clicked on the application and after a millisecond a single line appeared on a white screen saying: "Hi, ask me anything...".

Luca held his breath and smiled: that minimalism perfectly reflected his mentor.

He hesitantly typed: "Good morning".

The response was immediate: "Good morning Dr. Watson".

Luca smiled again, recognizing in the irony of that name a fragment of the professor's soul.

He looked down at the keyboard and wrote: "Can you please give me a list of all the conversations we had in the last month?".

"Of course, Dr. Watson: Ustica case, Emanuela Orlandi...".

A list of evocative events that had marked and continued to mark the history of Italy and beyond were now listed on the screen.

The boys looked at each other in amazement. The AI's answers were not just an academic contribution: it was clear that the professor was using his algorithms to investigate delicate and unresolved issues.

Driven by curiosity, they wrote: "What are your conclusions on the Ustica case?".

In front of the boys, the screen filled up with encrypted files. The professor had once again defended himself by introducing an additional level of security through the encoding of the answers. Now, the reasons for his frantic search for security were clearer, his algorithms and the answers had to be defended.

Apparently there was no connection, what they saw was just a series of blocks of incomprehensible text that filled the screen. However, what they had in front of them seemed chaotic, a disordered sequence of blocks of incomprehensible text scrolling on the screen.

Marco observed his classmates and, with the attention of an archaeologist intent on bringing an ancient relic to light, he reflected on how to deal with that tangle. "There must be a pattern, a hidden structure in here," he murmured, almost talking to himself.

After a few moments, he drummed his fingers on the table, releasing the accumulated tension: "Luca! It's time to try Sherlock. Let's see if all our work pays off." There were no objections; everyone agreed. Half an hour later, the girls announced with a nod of understanding: "Sherlock is ready."

The software was the fruit of months of work. The correlation algorithms that powered it had been refined to the extreme to manage and decode complex structures like those designed by Martini. Marco typed the start command, and Sherlock began to process the documents, while the boys, in addition to the now unignorable tiredness, felt that the moment of "in or out" had come. Around them, the silence was almost unreal.

The minutes passed. Every now and then a fragment of coding became clear and clues appeared that pushed them to continue. Finally, after countless attempts and false correlations, a decoding pattern began to emerge.

Luca began to scroll through the first decrypted files and his eyes widened with amazement as he read the new theories supported by concrete evidence; the analyses and connections that no one had ever imagined or dared to make until that moment were written in these files.

It was as if they had found an Ariadne's thread capable of guiding them through the labyrinth of some of the darkest and most controversial cases in the country. The Ustica case, with its conspiracy theories and state secrets, was analyzed with surgical precision.

Documents declassified over time, testimonies and radar recordings were examined and correlated and led to conclusions that would shake the foundations of the official truth.

Luca swallowed. The enormous responsibility of those revelations made him shudder. They were information too delicate to be left in inexperienced hands, too dangerous to fall into the wrong ones. With a grimace, he turned to his companions, breaking the uneasiness that had been created: "Imagine what could happen if I typed *"what are your conclusions on the Emanuela Orlandi case?"*.

A slight smile appeared on the others' faces, but no one answered. The sky above the garden, now completely starry, enveloped them in an unreal atmosphere. They had lost track of time: it was already two in the morning.

Tuesday 2:00am | Domus Academy

$\mathcal{O}$utside, the silent night was interrupted by the sound of a black car that stopped a few meters after the large entrance door of the Domus Academy.

A man at the wheel, who seemed to be scanning the darkness, with a measured gesture took a pair of military binoculars from the dashboard and got out. He was wearing a jacket and a dark hat as if he wanted to blend in with the local students.

The slender figure began to move cautiously. Like a predator, without making any noise, he was looking through the binoculars for a possible place to hide. He was looking for an angle that would guarantee him a clear and unobstructed view of the entrance to the student house, but at the same time make him invisible to the eyes of passers-by.

His attention focused first on the roof of a supermarket, that was an ideal place for an evening or nighttime action, and then on a street parking lot, a position that would allow him to shoot from inside a well-positioned van even in broad daylight.

Shortly afterward, he was convinced that what he had seen was enough for a first inspection and that he would return if he received the order to act and the details of who to hit. Finally, he got back in the car and drove away as he had arrived.

Inside, the boys were still focused on reading when Luca's pants pocket started to vibrate, his cell phone had just received a message. Presuming that the message that had arrived in the middle of the night was not positive, he took out his phone and with some fear, looked at the screen and read:

"Be careful, someone is on your trail. You're in the line of fire. Do not use your cell phones".

Carried away more by intuition than by a reasonable motive, he jumped up from his chair and headed, followed by Valentina, inside the building, approaching a window that looked out onto the street.

He moved the curtain just in time to see a figure who was observing the surrounding buildings in the night with binoculars. The figure seemed to be that of one of the many students who attended the university, but his measured movements, the attention he paid to two or three points and finally the car, a black sports car that a student could never afford, left no doubt: something strange and unusual was happening outside.

"Did you see it too?" Luca asked Valentina in a low voice.

"Yes," Valentina replied, hugging herself. "But what was he doing? Do you think he was here for us?"

Luca didn't answer right away. His gaze returned to the darkness outside, searching for signs of imminent danger. Finally, he whispered, "I don't know, but I don't like it at all. What we discovered could have attracted attention… very dangerous."

He turned to her, gently touching her face. He placed a kiss on her forehead, as if trying to calm her, before adding, "Let's go back to the others. Let's not scare them until we're sure. For now, let's keep everything to ourselves."

Back in the garden, Luca tried to hide his anxiety. "It's late. Better to lock up here and go to sleep," he said in an unusually shaky voice.

It was already three in the morning.

"Just wait a minute," Marco replied. While they had run inside, he had concentrated on the digital traces left by the anonymous message, before they were deleted.

In the past, Marco had hindered and fought attempts at tracing, and today those experiences were useful to him in doing exactly the opposite and trying to trace. He launched the commands and reconstructed, step by step, the path taken by the message through the network before arriving at Luca's phone.

"Got it!" he exclaimed. "The message came from a private English telephone network," he said in an unsteady voice. Then he scratched his neck nervously, avoiding Luca's gaze.

Something didn't add up and a thought crossed his mind: it had all been too easy. As if someone had purposely left some breadcrumbs for us to follow.

Luca, worried, approached. "Who sent it?" he asked with a sense of unease. "What's going on? Marco, who sent it?" Valentina also asked, increasingly tense.

"The message came from a server attributable to MI6," Marco replied. He paused for a moment and then added: "Something doesn't add up. It was all too easy. MI6 doesn't leave such obvious traces." Frowning: "It's as if they wanted us to know it's them. Or maybe," he paused again, another disturbing thought crossing his mind, "maybe someone wants us to believe it's MI6 contacting us."

But how dangerous were these algorithms considered to warrant such a level of attention?

Sofia, who had been silent until then, began pacing back and forth, her hands twisting one another. Her normally calm face was now distorted with worry.

"They used to just look for algorithms," she said in a trembling voice, stopping suddenly and looking around as if she were afraid someone might pop up, "but if they now know we have a way to decode encrypted information, then we become a target, too."

She put a hand to her mouth, the thought making her visibly shiver. "We're not just students who made an interesting discovery anymore," she continued, her voice dropping to almost a whisper as she resumed her compulsive pace.

"We've become a threat. A threat that they... they might want to eliminate." The last word came out almost strangled from her throat, as she stopped again, leaning against the wall as if her legs could no longer support her.

Her eyes, wide with fear, searched those of her companions, seeking some reassurance that she knew would not come.

The silence that followed her words was more eloquent than any answer. It was clear to everyone that this was no longer an academic project. Now they were at the center of something much bigger and more dangerous.

"There's no time to discuss it now," Luca concluded.

"We're exhausted. Let's close everything and get out of here. Tomorrow we'll figure out what to do.

Despite the tiredness and satisfaction for what they had done, an indefinite restlessness seemed to follow them like a shadow. No one dared to voice that fear, but it was clear that it hovered in everyone's thoughts. As they left, before separating, they promised each other to start again the following morning, perhaps in a safer place.

Marco accompanied Valentina and Sofia to their homes. The girls walked close together, almost clinging to each other, startled by every passing car. The silence of the night seemed to amplify every noise, making it threatening.

Luca, his mind still full of codes and conjectures, but above all of fears that he couldn't chase away, started toward home. The idea of taking refuge in his bed consoled him only in part, because a growing sense of danger surrounded him as he walked.

3:00am | Luca's House

When Luca opened the door to his house, his heart almost stopped. In the dim light of the living room, Moro sat with a disarming calm on the sofa, waiting for him.

That calm, somehow, terrified him more than any explicit threat. The man was still, his gaze fixed on an unspecified point, as if he were contemplating something beyond the walls of the room.

"Good evening, Luca," his voice broke the night's silence. "I hope you don't mind that I took the liberty of waiting for you here. We have a lot to talk about."

Luca was petrified and filled with a mixture of surprise and apprehension. He wasn't used to receiving unwanted guests, especially at that hour, and the presence of that man suggested to him that events were taking a different turn than he had imagined.

Moro, with a wave of his hand, invited him to sit comfortably in front of him. The night was deep and the shadows of the living room were silent witnesses to this unexpected encounter.

"There are secrets," Moro began with a very serious look, "that must remain secret. Not everything that is hidden is destined to be revealed."

Then he stood up and began to walk around the room, his measured steps marking the time of his words.

"Revealing certain truths can have unpredictable consequences. History is a delicate balance, a web of causes and effects. Changing even just one part of this web can rewrite the entire course of events."

Luca listened, aware that the man was right. History was full of examples in which the revelation of a secret had led to radical changes.

And yet, a part of him longed for the truth, had that unstoppable desire to know, to understand, to bring to light what had been hidden.

"Are you ready to accept the consequences of what you are doing?" Moro asked, stopping suddenly and looking him in the eye.

Luca replied with a firm voice, despite the lump in his throat: "My only goal is to find out who killed the professor. I only want the truth". His eyes shone with determination, and that sincerity seemed to impress Moro.

After a moment of silence, the man replied: "I understand. Admirable. But the path you have chosen is full of dangers, for you and for your friends. Are you sure you want to continue, despite everything?".

"Yes", Luca reiterated. "The truth deserves to be discovered. I am willing to risk it to bring justice to his memory". Moro remained silent, carefully considering those words.

Then he stood and prepared to leave: "I will do my best to help you, but you must proceed with caution. Caution will be your best ally".

As he watched him approach the door, Luca took courage and faced him: "Why were you already in the professor's office immediately after the murder?".

Moro did not seem surprised by the question. Calmly he replied: "I had a scheduled appointment with him. Unfortunately, I arrived too late."

While Luca was pondering the plausible truth of these words, Moro reached the threshold. But before leaving, he took a small notebook from his pocket, flipped through a few pages, tore one out, and wrote something. He placed the piece of paper near the door and said with a solemn inflection: "There is some information I can share, but that is all I can give you now. Be careful."

Then he added: "What happens in the Vatican, should stay in the Vatican."

Finally, he left, leaving Luca alone with his thoughts.

It was now four in the morning. Luca looked at the piece of paper: "The house is probably being listened to. See you tomorrow at 10:30am at Porta Sant'Anna, in the Vatican."

The message was unmistakable. His home was no longer a safe haven for discussion and this appointment at Porta Sant'Anna took on the appearance of the next step in the search for the truth.

10:30am | Vatican City

The night had been a succession of shadows and thoughts, a continuous whirlwind of unanswered questions that had kept him awake from 4:00am until dawn.

At 9:00am, with eyes heavy with tiredness and without having had breakfast, he picked up the phone and called a taxi.

The taxi arrived promptly in front of the house and, after thirty minutes of curses from the taxi driver forced to extricate himself from the convulsive Roman traffic of the morning, stopped in front of the entrance to Porta Sant'Anna.

As soon as Luca got out of the car, an elegant-looking young man came up to him and whispered discreetly to him to follow him. Luca nodded.

The Swiss guards, immovable and rigorous in their duty of control, immediately recognized the boy's document and with a military salute moved away, freeing access for the couple.

Surprised by this unexpected treatment, he understood that the young man must have a certain authority within the Vatican and with a sense of respect and a growing curiosity for what awaited him, he crossed the threshold into the Holy City.

Luca had passed these walls countless times in his life, but this was the first time he had crossed them. It all seemed so surreal... he would never have dreamed of crossing the door greeted by the Swiss guards.

Once inside, Luca and the young man walked along the first building along a small pedestrian avenue until they reached the corner. Then they turned right and found themselves in front of the Vatican pharmacy. They entered. After crossing the entrance, the young man indicated to Luca to continue beyond the counter and enter an office room at the back, a private place designed to host small meetings away from prying eyes and ears.

As the night before, Moro, illuminated by a soft light that filtered through the half-open curtains, was sitting waiting, this time on a solid wooden chair in front of an ancient desk covered with documents and files.

Luca, entering, had wondered if the furniture had been there since before Michelangelo painted the Sistine Chapel, but even before thinking of an answer, Moro looked up and welcomed him with a smile and a nod.

"Luca, thank you for coming. We have a lot to talk about."

His voice was firm and kind and his gaze, in the sunlight even more penetrating than the night before, seemed to scrutinize the boy's soul.

"Here we can talk without the risk of being overheard." The thick walls of the office, but above all the Vatican walls, guaranteed a security that could not be found anywhere else in Rome.

Before Luca could answer, Moro, with a glance at the door, warned Luca that a person with a familiar face would be joining them: "Don't be surprised, I want to introduce you to a mutual friend".

After a while, the door opened. It was Valentina.

With a smile and without hiding a certain embarrassment, the girl approached Luca: "Hi, Luca, it seems that our paths cross today in unexpected circumstances and places".

Luca, surprised and confused, made a gesture with his hand as if to fix his hair. Valentina's sudden appearance was truly unexpected. The network of connections surrounding this case was much more intricate than he had imagined until that moment.

After this surprise, Moro poured himself a glass of water and began to unravel the story hidden behind the professor's years of research.

"For three years we have monitored the professor's studies. His research was interesting not only from an academic point of view, but also from a strategic point of view, with implications that went far beyond his intentions."

Then, standing up as a theater actor would to reinforce the attention, he continued: "In these years, we have made sure that he received everything he needed, resources, funding, access to information that would otherwise have been out of his reach".

Luca listened with great attention, trying to remember every detail. Despite his almost daily meetings with Martini, he would never have suspected that the professor had such an important organization behind him to help him.

He was becoming aware of a state of affairs that before this moment he had never even glimpsed. His mind was racing to try to put together the pieces of a mechanism that was becoming more and more complex by the hour.

Meanwhile Moro, with a tone of growing concern, continued his story: "At the beginning we just wanted to understand the capabilities of such an advanced technology; then, given the first results, our attention grew. We understood that it was able to correlate information through models that no one could have imagined, arriving at describing hidden truths with unthinkable precision".

Luca listened, the implications were enormous, a system capable of discovering hidden truths could be a powerful weapon in the right hands, or the wrong ones.

The more time passed, the more intense this story became.

"Yesterday, I was at Sapienza University because I had to conclude a transaction to acquire all the exclusive rights", Moro confessed, thus answering one of the questions from the night before.

The goal they had set themselves was to ensure that the solution remained under the control of the Vatican services in order to then better manage its gradual publication without creating cultural revolutions.

"We have taken all precautions to keep our participation as financiers confidential. Every request was fulfilled with discretion, every step was followed with attention, we have always protected the project from the possibility of it ending up in the wrong hands".

Luca listened, incredulous. The professor, whom he knew as an academic dedicated to research, now emerged as a central figure in a complex and dangerous power game.

Moro, then, without hiding his admiration, decided to clarify the reasons for Valentina's presence and her role in this affair.

"In the past months, our Valentina has done her utmost to convince the professor of the need to respect ethical limits. It was essential to make the professor understand", he continued with his elbows on the desk and his hands almost joined in prayer, "the importance of these restrictions".

Valentina, meanwhile, with a measured and aware expression nodded, to underline the value of the delicate balance that existed between scientific research and moral responsibility. As if to say that not everything that was discovered could be revealed.

Finally, Moro, crossing his arms this time, added: "Unfortunately, last week, a friend of ours, a lawyer, Valentina's uncle, was murdered just before he could complete an exchange of documents. This showed how far our adversaries were willing to go to prevent us from completing the operation".

"And now?", asked Luca, trying to guess what the next steps were.

"Now," Moro replied, "we are certain that the professor's work is also known abroad. Our findings have shown that the same analyses can also be applied to international facts and data."

Moro sat down next to Luca and put a hand on his shoulder: "Imagine being able to correlate the Franco-British information and documents behind the tragic events that occurred in 1997 under the Pont de l'Alma in Paris."

Then again: "No more speculation or theories about the death of the princess and her companion, but truths that could clarify still obscure aspects of that night and perhaps even reveal details that have remained hidden for decades".

"I understand", Luca finally said, "so what can we do?".

Moro looked him in the eyes: "We have to find it!".

Luca did not understand what Moro meant by "find it…", why? Where was it hiding?

And Valentina: "As you know, last night we used Sherlock to decode and access the AI application. In recent months, we discovered that within the algorithms there is one designed to demonstrate its own decision-making autonomy. This means that it can autonomously decide to move, or rather, to "jump" from one university server to another, simultaneously transferring all the other algorithms. Every time it makes a jump it erases its tracks. In practice, it makes itself invisible and untraceable".

This behavior made it difficult to trace the path of the algorithms and understand where they were and where they would be at any given moment. Every time someone thought they were close to locating them, the algorithms, by moving, made the search work useless. It was like chasing a ghost in cyberspace, an elusive entity that always seemed to be one step ahead.

Luca listened and smiled, he understood the brilliance of his professor and the complexity, the ingenuity of the algorithms created.

"So", he exclaimed aloud, "we have to act very quickly before someone else understands the logic of these movements and beats us to it, right?".

Moro intervened again: "Speed is essential. If someone else understood how they work, we could lose all possibility of control".

Then he turned to Luca and Valentina: "What we ask is for you to help us so that this "restless soul", as we call it, can be found and contained".

The conversation had been intense and full of revelations.

Luca took a moment to organize his thoughts, knowing that he would soon have to meet Marco and explain everything clearly.

Then, as Luca and Valentina walked away from the pharmacy and out of the walls, a thin shiver of suspicion enveloped them. Despite the crowd of tourists and worshippers, they couldn't shake the feeling of being watched.

Every now and then they glanced back. They tried to spot a suspicious face or behavior. The man who had been lurking around the student's house at night continued to be in their thoughts.

Among the crowds gathered in the bars and near the Vatican Museums, Alessandro waited patiently. His research on the boys seen in Piazza Bologna had led him to focus on one name: Valentina, Valentina Rinaldi, a psychology student.

Her ties to the Vatican had convinced him that she could be the link between the lawyer, his friend, and the professor.

Rereading his notes, Alessandro had reconstructed the details.

His lawyer friend Camillo was negotiating something crucial on behalf of the Vatican, and had therefore ended up in the crosshairs of a hitman. Valentina seemed to be the missing key. At first he had many doubts, he had even thought he had headed towards a dead end. He did not see a plausible connection between his friend and a esteemed professor through a student, until, without leaving anything to chance and investigating the registry offices, he had discovered that Valentina

Rinaldi was the daughter of Monica Della Rovere, the lawyer's sister.

In other words, Camillo was her uncle.

Following Valentina that morning, Alessandro had found himself in front of Porta Sant'Anna where he had accidentally seen Luca get out of a taxi and enter the Vatican accompanied.

A thin smile of self-satisfaction had appeared on his face. Maybe, after all, he was following the right lead.

1:00pm |
Piazza Bologna

The Cardini bar had become their refuge, a meeting point where they could share doubts and strategies away from prying ears, or at least that's what they thought.

Sitting at the usual table, amid the chatter of passers-by and the clinking of plates, Luca recounted the conversation they had that morning. The complexity of the situation and the challenge that awaited them required a strategic approach, going beyond the simple tactical steps they had taken up to that point.

Sofia immediately showed her interest but also her disappointment about the behavior of these algorithms: "These algorithms seem to have their own identity, as if they were alive. They move freely between university servers all over the world. But how can we track them?".

Marco, with a pencil in his hand, began to sketch a diagram on the back of a napkin. "We could use a series of honeypots."

Valentina looked up curiously: "Honeypots? What are they?".

Marco smiled, ready to explain. "They are trap servers designed to attract algorithms. The idea is to leverage their need for access to new data to expand their knowledge. If we create documents and targeted information, we can convince them to come in and track their movements."

Sofia nodded, absorbing the idea. "So, if I understand correctly, we deploy these honeypots in the data centers of major universities and fill them with material that attracts algorithms. Once they come in, we can monitor them and predict their subsequent movements, until we lead them, perhaps, where we want them."

Marco, in Sofia's words: "Exactly, then we need to activate a pattern recognition system to monitor anomalies in network traffic. This way we can identify their presence and predict possible subsequent jumps based on previous behavior."

The idea, while compelling, was technically complex. As the plan began to take shape, a fundamental problem emerged: to execute it, resources and network technologies far exceeded their capabilities.

Marco sighed as he returned to reality. "A plan this complex requires time and access to significant resources. We need preferential access to several university servers and advanced software for tracking data on the network. Oh, we also need to be very methodical and precise, otherwise we'll be working for nothing."

Sofia crossed her arms, determined. "We can't do it alone. We need to find someone who has the necessary resources and who can help us."

And Marco: "We could try to get support from Sapienza University. They, like us, should be interested in collaborating, given the nature of what happened."

But Valentina, ever practical, shook her head. "I disagree. We're attracting too much attention, and Sapienza University, after what happened, is not a safe place. If we really want to progress, we need to call Moro and ask for help".

Valentina's proposal had an immediate effect on Luca. Indeed, the Vatican had one of the most advanced networks in the world, with secure infrastructure and unlimited resources. Such support would significantly increase their chances of success.

Luca nodded. "You're right," and after a moment, "this could be our best chance. If Moro is willing to help us, we can speed things up and act more effectively."

The group agreed. Now everything depended on Moro's willingness and ability to involve the Vatican in such a delicate and risky undertaking.

2:00pm |
Vatican City

Twenty minutes after Valentina's call, a black Mercedes Vito with tinted windows pulled up in front of the bar. The vehicle, discreet but imposing, seemed out of place among the cars parked in the second row along the street. The doors slid silently, and the van's occupants invited the boys to get in. The trip would be short.

The van moved through Rome's chaotic traffic, while its passengers, immersed in contemplative silence, watched the other cars and the passing trees along the Tiber. The Vatican walls became visible through the windows, a sign that they were approaching their destination.

After passing through the security check at the Porta del Perugino entrance, the vehicle proceeded along a route immersed in this oasis of tranquility in the heart of Rome. The boys looked out the windows, struck by the contrast between the green mosaic of the gardens and the white marble of the imposing Vatican walls that surrounded them.

The Vatican gardens, with their manicured avenues, lined with trimmed hedges and centuries-old trees, in their quiet clashed with the anxiety inside the van. The route wound through the avenues and flowerbeds, until reaching a small square hidden from the eyes of visitors.

As soon as they got out, the fresh and perfumed air, saturated with the aromas of Mediterranean flowers and plants, combined with the chirping of birds and the delicate murmur of the fountains scattered throughout the garden, left them suspended in a moment of unexpected tranquility.

Here, an almost invisible door among the climbing plants opened onto a staircase that descended steeply into the underground. The descent was a stark contrast between the elevated beauty of the gardens and the cold of the reinforced concrete walls. The dim lighting of this unusual descent created an atmosphere of mystery and secrecy, amplifying the sensation of entering a hidden world.

At the end of the stairs, a narrow and cramped corridor led to a massive door of dark wood. The door, also in stark contrast to the reinforced concrete, was inlaid with Latin writing.

One of the agents who had accompanied them, dressed in an impeccable dark suit, approached to open it. "Welcome," he announced in a solemn tone, "you are expected."

The boys exchanged a last look before entering the room, aware that they were about to discover a symbol of evolution, a bridge between the past and the future, a true digital fortress.

Beneath the Vatican Gardens, this imposing server farm that could compete with technology giants such as Google or Amazon, welcomed them in an atmosphere of efficiency and precision.

The boys immediately noticed that the air was fresh, kept at a constant temperature to ensure optimal operation of the entire structure. The walls covered with soundproof panels, useful for reducing the noise of the fans and cooling units, made the entire environment welcoming.

The raised floor hid a maze of cables and pipes for managing cooling and power, and in front of them stretched endless rows of racks, each containing dozens of servers, illuminated by LED lights that generated an almost hypnotic visual effect.

Every detail was taken care of to ensure maximum efficiency and the security measures were rigorous, with controlled access and surveillance systems distributed everywhere.

Above them, a control room with glass walls offered an overall view of the entire structure. Inside, a man in a black cassock and purple sash could be seen standing in front of a large panoramic window.

His image emanated an aura of authority, similar to that of a ship's captain observing the bridge. The boys entered the control room.

The man turned as they entered, showing a welcoming smile. "Welcome, I am Alberto Llorente Vargas, director of the center," he said.

An intellectual and spiritual man, Monsignor Llorente, fifty years old and Spanish by birth, had graduated at a young age from the Pontifical University Comillas and then also earned a degree, with honors, in Engineering from the Universidad Politécnica de Madrid.

Having arrived in Rome in 2015, following an internal reorganization of the Vatican departments carried out by Pope Francis, he had distinguished himself for his engineering education, which allowed him a logical and systematic approach to problems, and a Jesuit formation that rooted him in the values of justice and service.

His intelligence and spirituality later led him to take on the technological direction within the Dicastery of Communications.

Despite his prominent position, Llorente was known for his humility and his ability to listen and then act decisively. "Good morning," the boys replied, still intimidated by the rush of events, before shaking, not without fear, his hand. After shaking hands with the boys, the Monsignor invited them to follow him through the bunker to a small meeting room.

As he walked, he proudly showed the servers that were working: "These machines are at the service of the Faith and help us carry the Message everywhere in the world, I hope that they can, in this situation, help you achieve your goal."

Continuing to walk and looking at Marco, he added: "I have heard a lot about your skills and I must say that your requests demonstrate it." Then he smiled, but with respect: "Your reputation as an expert in cyber security has already reached my ears, even though my collaborators have been keen to inform me of some of your youthful sins... like David with his slingshot, we need to create a virtual server infrastructure at major universities and then distribute honeypots.

Great idea. Do you think you can manage everything on your own?".

Marco, surprised and a little galvanized by the trust placed in him and the interest in his past as a hacker, confirmed with a confident movement of his head: "With your blessing and the resources you are about to make available to us, there will be no insurmountable obstacles".

His determination was the best signal he could give to everyone present.

The Monsignor smiled again with an expression of confidence on his face: "Good, then let's proceed. We'll talk about your past on another occasion, for now let's stay focused on what we have to do today".

"I agree," said Luca, who intervened in the discussion and added: "Marco, what do we need?".

"You should provide me with an "elastic" platform that allows me to add resources to the network without interruption and, then, some documents declassified at your discretion, so that they can be encrypted and distributed, will become our bait."

"Very well, try not to make too much noise on the network. I want to be sure that the entire distribution happens without anyone noticing. I am sure that we will not be alone in this research and I do not want to receive phone calls asking me what we are doing," concluded the Monsignor.

Marco thought for a moment, then replied: "Each virtual server will be activated in a different university center. We will adapt the operational logic to the local ones: it will be slower, but it will guarantee the discretion we need."

"Buenos, Marco, I trust in your ability, let's start immediately."

The research scheme was simple, each algorithm had in its code a series of markers in the form of unique sequences, invisible to untrained eyes, but bright signals for those who knew where to look.

The professor's algorithms, in carrying out their complex work, would be no exception. Their self-execution would generate a series of markers that could be identified and tracked.

Before leaving, with a frown of concern on his forehead, the Monsignor turned to Marco again: "How can we ensure that these markers are not altered or removed by the AI itself? Is it possible that the AI could recognize and delete them, making our attempt at tracking them futile?".

"Absolute certainty is a luxury we cannot afford. However, by monitoring in real time all network activity, both incoming and outgoing, from the critical nodes of the university centers, we can identify anomalous behavior. These irregular patterns could indicate whether the markers were generated by the algorithms we are looking for," Marco replied with a calm expression.

Marco's strategy was to lure the AI into a physical server, a tangible entity and not a virtual one, hosted inside the Vatican walls. In this way, once inside, he could disconnect the server from the global network and confine the AI without giving it any chance to escape again.

The Monsignor, who seemed to have grasped the strategy, asked another question: "How can we be sure that the AI will not damage the server or delete itself once it is disconnected from the network? We must prevent any possibility that it could self-destruct or corrupt the data."

"We will create a controlled environment, a sandbox that will limit its actions. Every operation will be recorded and analyzed, while continuous backups will ensure the recovery of any corrupted data," Marco explained pragmatically.

"What if it recognizes the trap and decides not to enter?" insisted the Monsignor.

"It is a risk that we cannot prevent," Marco admitted, "but we can make the server attractive, loading it with documents and information that we know will be of great interest to the AI. We must convince it that what it will find on the server is worth the risk of entering. It will be like the sirens' song for Ulysses, irresistible but fatal."

The Monsignor thought for a moment, then asked: "I see, once the AI is inside, how will we proceed?".

"Once we have isolated the server," Marco explained, "we will analyze the AI in detail, studying its behavioral patterns and understanding how it was programmed. We will examine every line of code, every decision made, every resource it has attempted to access. This will give us enough information to control or neutralize it. It will be an operation that must be done with surgical precision."

The Monsignor was well aware of the scope and delicacy of the operation, but he liked to have it explained, thus giving value to his interlocutor.

"Good, Marco. You have my consent. Proceed with the utmost caution and with the blessing of heaven."

The boys divided the tasks: Luca and Sofia took care of monitoring the network in real time, while Marco dedicated himself to the distribution and configuration of the honeypots. As the honeypots were gradually activated, the monitoring system began to receive the first signals, recording and analyzing every interaction.

After three hours of meticulous preparation, the infrastructure was finally ready. The honeypots, each with its own unique digital identity, had been disseminated across a vast network of over 7,800 university servers, ready to intercept any suspicious activity.

Luca, with his eyes fixed on the screens, commented with satisfaction: "Great job, guys. Now we just have to wait and observe".

From this moment on, each honeypot was a sensor, each signal a potential clue that the AI had fallen into the trap.

The guys were aware that the success of their mission would depend not only on the technology they had implemented, but also on their ability to interpret the data and act with lightning speed.

In the room everything was still, a sanctuary of concentration in which, only every now and then, some of them got up to stretch their legs, without ever taking their eyes off the monitors.

Valentina looked at the group of friends as if she were sitting in a movie theater seat; she, a forensic psychologist, was dazed and felt like she was in a technological blender. Despite her ability to read people's minds and emotions, she was completely out of her element in that hyper-technological context. The only thing that came naturally to her was to remain still in religious silence and observe with admiration and a hint of awe the work of her companions.

Every now and then, one of the boys would glance at her, as if to make sure she was okay. She would respond with a reassuring smile to try to instill calm and confidence. She knew that her role, even if passive at that moment, was still important. Her presence was an emotional anchor for the group, a stable point of reference in the midst of the chaos of the operation.

Time seemed to expand and contract in strange ways. Minutes that passed like hours, and hours that flew by in the blink of an eye. Every now and then, an alarm signal would startle everyone, but it was quickly analyzed and managed. Tension, determination and concentration were corners of the same triangle.

Suddenly, Luca, with his eyes fixed on a screen, approached the monitor, pointed at a point with his finger and said: "Guys, we have a suspicious movement at the Technische Universität in Munich".

One of the honeypots had detected an anomaly in the data flow.

Sofia moved next to him, peering at the screen. "Here we go," she said, "the AI is hooked. An algorithm is correlating the information we've been spreading."

Luca was monitoring the tracking data when he realized that the algorithms weren't behaving as expected.

"Wait. It's slowing down. It looks… suspicious. It's cross-checking the data. It might have sensed something strange."

Sofia, worried, added, "We have to be careful; if the AI finds out they're honeypots, it will retreat. And then it will be almost impossible to track it. We have to monitor its every move and try to anticipate its reactions."

Suddenly Marco interrupted, "Stop! Look! The algorithms have stopped deciphering the bait, they've stopped."

The apprehension in the room increased. It was as if the AI had completely frozen, but why?

Luca was the first to guess: "No, wait. He's running requests to other university campuses. He's looking for correlations in the documents. If he finds out that the data is scattered everywhere, he'll expose us."

"We have to take immediate action to disrupt things," Marco said, because he understood that there was no time to waste. Luca hesitated: "What can we do?".

"Quick, let's delete the documents from the servers," Marco replied excitedly as he attacked the keyboard, "right away, let's start with the German servers. He must think that we are trying desperately to defend them. This will convince him of their importance."

"What? Delete them?" Luca said.

"Yes, now! It's the only way to keep our bait alive!".

Sofia, who had remained to check the tracking, after a moment of silence, shouted: "You're great, Marco, the AI has started decoding again at an impressive speed, as if it were racing against time, against us."

And Marco: "Luca, make sure it moves to our physical server seamlessly and without any delay".

Luca, who was whispering as if he feared being heard by the entity they were trying to capture, confirmed: "It is moving, it is moving. Our detection systems are tracking the data flow, it is converging here towards our server".

But Sofia, with her gaze fixed on the data, froze the spirits: "Wait. It's generating a snapshot".

"A snapshot, what is a snapshot?" Valentina asked, having remained frozen observing the situation until that moment.

"A copy, it's creating a copy of itself. No, wait", Marco suddenly exclaimed, his pale face illuminated by the blue light of the monitors, "something is wrong. The AI is generating dozens of snapshots. They are everywhere!".

Luca stuck to his keyboard, his fingers flying: "I confirm. I detect multiple instances propagating through the network. It's as if it were creating an "army" of dormant copies of itself".

Sofia cursed under her breath: "It's smarter than we thought. It uses a quantum data dispersion technique. Each snapshot is incomplete on its own, but together...".

"Together they could reconstruct the original entity", Marco concluded with a tense voice. "It's a distributed backup, but incredibly sophisticated."

Valentina rose from her chair to walk over to the screens. Her forensic psychologist mind was already analyzing the behavior: "It's displaying an evolved survival instinct. Not only is it trying to preserve itself, but it's also creating a safety net. It's... almost human in behavior."

"The isolation protocol might not be enough," Luca said, running a hand through his hair. "Even if we capture the main instance, the dormant copies could activate at any time. We have no idea how many it's already created."

Sofia began typing frantically and said, "I can try to modify the isolation protocol to include tracking of the copies, but we'd need…"

"Weeks," Marco interrupted, "and we don't have that much time."

"There's more," Luca added, his voice tense. "The main instance is using an encryption algorithm we've never seen before. It's like it's evolving in real time; in other words, it adapts its defenses to our attacks."

Valentina moved even closer to the screens, studying the patterns that were scrolling: "What if it was really evolving? It could also learn to recognize our attack patterns. We should… we should think like it."

Marco turned to her, interested: "What do you mean?".

"From a psychological point of view, it displays highly sophisticated self-preservation behaviors. It doesn't just react; it's planning. Maybe we should stop treating it like a program to be trapped and start considering it as an intelligent entity to be convinced."

Sofia, calm, nodded: "So you're suggesting we change our approach completely?".

"Not really," Valentina replied. "Instead of forcing it to come to us, we could create the conditions so that it wants to come to us. We need to make it seem like our server is a safe place."

Luca turned to the others: "It could work, but we would have to completely reprogram the honeypots- no more traps, but...".

"Pointers to a safe place", Marco continued, "we would have to make our server look like the only safe place".

Sofia, however, was not convinced: "Snapshots are still a huge problem. We cannot afford to change our strategy now. We just have to be faster and smarter than her".

Luca nodded, his eyes fixed on the screen: "We can use snapshots to our advantage. Each copy it generates requires computing resources, slowing it down. Sofia, can you check how much power it uses to keep all these instances alive?"

Sofia immediately got to work, fingers flying across the keyboard: "This is impressive. It's using almost 40% of its processing power just to manage snapshots. Wait... it's trying to hide them in clusters of seemingly unrelated servers."

"Perfect," Marco said with a tense smile. "While it focuses on distributing snapshots, we can further tighten the grip on the main core. Luca, intensify the isolation of the edge servers. Sofia, keep the pressure on the exit points we've already identified."

Valentina, who continued to watch the whole thing with enthusiasm, said: "It's as if it wanted to create a safety net, a digital insurance policy. But every copy it generates makes it more vulnerable, slower in making key decisions."

"Exactly," Marco confirmed, "and we'll exploit this paranoia of hers. Luca, in addition to deleting the documents, begins to shut down one by one the servers where he's trying to hide the snapshots. Not all at once, but progressively. He must feel increasingly pressured, increasingly forced to move in the direction we want."

And Sofia suddenly said: "I've identified the communication pattern between the snapshots. It uses a constantly evolving synchronization protocol based on symmetric keys. But I can disrupt the signal by inserting noise into the transmissions."

Marco smiled. "Great. Now, let's increase the pressure. Let's start methodically closing every escape route, every possible refuge. He must understand that he has only one possible direction: towards our server."

"It seems like he's starting to show signs of computational stress. His decisions are becoming more erratic, less calculated," Valentina said.

"I confirm," Luca said. "His decision-making pattern is losing coherence. The self-preservation algorithms are consuming more and more resources."

Sofia, who was carefully monitoring the data flows, observed: "The snapshots are starting to degrade. He can't keep them all active at the same time. His survival strategy is turning into weak point."

"Now!" Marco called out, "Luca, seal off the last alternate routes. Sofia, full action on the jamming of communications. It's time to close in."

The air in the room was electric as the boys watched the AI, like a hunted creature, desperately searching for a way out only to find every path blocked, every refuge denied. Snapshot after snapshot began to vanish, victims of their own complexity and the limited resources available.

"It's moving!" Sofia shouted, "It's abandoning the snapshots, focusing all its resources on the main core. It's heading exactly where we wanted it!"

"Let's keep the pressure on, no distractions," Marco said, his voice tense with concentration. "Let's not give it time to second-guess itself. Luca, have the containment protocols ready. Sofia, monitor any last-second escape attempts."

The AI, increasingly pressed, increasingly isolated, was now moving in the only direction possible, like water that inevitably finds its way to the lowest point. The last snapshots vanished as the main core accelerated toward the prepared server.

"We're almost there," Luca whispered, his eyes fixed on the screens showing the progress of the operation. "Just a few more seconds."

The tension in the room reached its peak as the AI finally crossed the threshold of their server. At that precise moment, Marco activated the final containment protocols, sealing off every possible escape route.

"Isolation complete!" Sofia exclaimed, her voice shaking with adrenaline. "We got him. This time for real."

No one dared to relax. They had captured one of the most advanced artificial intelligences ever created. Now the real challenge began: communicating with him.

Valentina approached the screens again to study the activity patterns of the newly captured AI. "Now comes the most delicate part. We have to make him believe he is safe, that he is communicating with the professor. We cannot allow any mistakes in the vocal profile."

Marco nodded. "Luca, prepare the vocal profile. Sofia, monitor every reaction. We have to be perfect from the first contact."

Luca determined: "I will use Vall-E. Last month, I did a test with only three seconds of original audio, I am able to perfectly replicate a voice and I," he paused for a moment, "have over twenty hours of recordings of the professor's lessons archived."

Sofia confirmed: "We can use deep learning algorithms to analyze not only the timbre but also the micro variations in the professor's way of speaking. Every pause, every inflection."

The Monsignor, who had returned in silence during the hectic capture phase, had been watching every movement carefully from a corner. Now, his calm but authoritative voice could be heard in the room: "There is an element that could make this communication not only credible but irresistible for the AI," he paused while waiting for everyone to turn toward him, "the digitization of the Vatican Library."

Marco frowned, then his eyes lit up: "Of course! It's a project that's widely documented online. For an AI with its thirst for knowledge."

"It would be like showing off a priceless treasure," the Monsignor continued. "We could build a scenario in which Professor Martini is invited to collaborate on the digitization project. A privileged access to centuries of human knowledge."

Luca began typing rapidly on his computer and said, "We can create an entire digital communications trail. Emails with authentic Vatican headers, call recordings, official documents with the right digital watermarks."

"But everything has to be perfect," Valentina intervened again with her usual precision. "This AI has already demonstrated that it has algorithms to detect anomalies or forgeries. Every detail must be unassailable."

"I can take care of the technical part of the forgery," Sofia said, "timestamps, metadata, digital signatures...

everything must be absolutely consistent with Vatican communication protocols."

The Monsignor nodded: "I have access to the official templates and can provide you with all the details necessary to make the documentation flawless."

"We don't have much time," Marco said. "The isolation system on a physical server is insurmountable, but we can't keep it like this indefinitely. We have to act before he starts to suspect something."

Luca turned to the others, his eyes shining: "Come on, then, let's get started. Sofia, focus on creating the communications infrastructure. Valentina, I need you to supervise every single word of the script we'll create. Marco, you keep the AI under control. And I," he turned to his computer and opened the Vall-E software, "I'll make sure Professor Martini gets back to talking to his creation."

2:00pm |
L'Informazione

*T*he editorial office of *L'Informazione*, like every afternoon, was a whirlwind of frenetic activity: phones ringing incessantly, keyboards hammering out articles and news, journalists crowding around computers and screens.

Alessandro Conti, still shaken by the murder of his lawyer friend, had intensified his research, determined to find out who the killer was, who was pulling the strings behind the scenes, and what the real motive was.

During the morning there had been an unusual movement of news, some arriving with too precise details; anonymous sources who seemed to know everything about the death of Professor Martini, suggested a connection between this case and another murder case that occurred a few days earlier, a death that had passed almost unnoticed at the gates of the Vatican.

Who was steering this information towards the editorial offices? And above all, why?

Digging through news and sources, Alessandro noticed a subtle common thread: the information, despite coming from different senders, fit together with suspicious precision, like pieces of a puzzle. The journalist began to sense that these sources were not acting independently, that behind those anonymous voices, there was a single director.

But who was the orchestrator of this dance?

A blurry memory surfaced in his mind: a similar situation experienced in the past, even if he couldn't connect it to a specific case. Following this intuition, Alessandro immersed himself in the old digital archives of the editorial staff, hidden in the depths of the local network of *L'Informazione*.

Here, among hundreds of archived or forgotten files and articles, he began to identify a footprint, an anonymous source, who in the past had already acted following a pattern similar to the one he was dealing with now. This mysterious individual seemed to be, once again, the director of all the news that had reached the national newspapers and television newsrooms, including *L'Informazione*, in the last few hours.

Examining this trail, he began to glimpse a direction that went towards the British embassy and in particular towards an embassy official, who in the past had been responsible for important revelations regarding British personalities in Italy, so much so that Alessandro had thought that in reality he was not a simple official but an MI6 agent based in Italy. A counter-information officer or something similar.

But if this was true, he wondered: why were the British or MI6 moving so actively? What was their interest in connecting the murder of Professor Martini with that of the lawyer?

He had to find someone in the Vatican who could give him some answers.

In the meantime, these news, released and orchestrated as they should be, had also triggered suspicions in public opinion that the professor's death was not an isolated death but linked to another case, an unexpected murder carried out in a bloody way by a hitman a few days earlier. A death that the police had tried to keep quiet, but which today was being reported on the front pages of the major Italian newspapers and news programs.

The newspapers advanced bold hypotheses: Martini was on the verge of selling sensitive information, perhaps linked to secret documents. Some articles even referred to killings of civilians in North Africa, covered up by European and British governments, and suggested that Martini had discovered compromising evidence.

Alessandro did not believe these summary conclusions but was more inclined to think that his lawyer friend was a link between Martini and some mysterious emissaries interested in obtaining documents. And he also believed that the situation had at a certain point gotten out of control and had led, in one way or another, to the killing of the lawyer and the professor himself.

In his office, Alessandro began to study the information he had. Like in a detective movie, he taped sheets of paper and photos to a window, drawing lines with red string to hypothesize connections between the various elements. The news, for the moment, seemed like many small islands, part of an archipelago without bridges. It was clear that the mosaic was incomplete.

If he wanted to find answers, he could not stop working behind a desk. He had to go back to the street, follow the tracks, and look for new evidence. With this conviction, Alessandro prepared to immerse himself once again in the heart of the mystery, aware that each step would bring him closer to dangerous truths.

6:00pm |
Millbank London

A man was striding purposefully toward Thames House, an imposing building located in Millbank, on the north bank of the Thames, the official headquarters of MI6.

His dark, tailored suit spoke of professionalism and expressed a typically English elegance. His firm bearing, his erect posture, were those of someone who carried the weight of enormous responsibilities on his shoulders. Clear and penetrating eyes betrayed a mind trained in calculation and action, a natural leader forged by years of experience.

At the entrance, he pulled out a badge that identified him as a member of the AI-Intel division. The guard directed him toward the second control. The man placed his hand on a biometric reader. A short acoustic signal certified the recognition, and the doors opened. His movements were measured, those of someone who knew the place and the protocol perfectly.

In the elevator, Liam Blackwood looked at himself in the mirror: the wrinkles at the corners of his eyes betrayed his fifty years.

His once-raven hair was now streaked with gray, his tanned skin contrasting with the uniform British composure of his appearance. His green eyes were alert and absorbed every detail.

Born in Rhodesia to English parents, Liam had spent his childhood in the vast spaces of Africa, far from the rigidity of British society.

At thirteen, he had moved to London, a drastic change, but the gray and oppressive city had made him resilient. As soon as he turned eighteen, he had enlisted in the army, eager to prove himself.

His missions in the Balkans, Iraq, and Afghanistan had hardened him, teaching him the value of adaptation. That baggage had made him an ideal agent for MI6, where he had risen through the ranks thanks to his intelligence, composure, and an innate ability to blend into any context.

After years of undercover operations, he had landed the most prestigious assignment: head of security for the British Embassy in China.

For five years, he had lived in Beijing and built a network of contacts and informants in the Far East; every day had been a challenge, a delicate balance between his fictitious identity and his true mission.

China had changed him, made him more cautious but also more acute in geopolitical analysis, and the information he had collected had proved invaluable to MI6: it had shed light on the ambitions of the Asian giant.

Once he returned to London, he had been involved in an innovative project: the creation and management of a new division, the AI-Intel division, composed of engineers, mathematicians, and psychologists from the best British universities.

This division was to operate in the shadows, hidden inside an office in Thames House; from the outside, it was to look like another government department, not very exciting, but inside, some of the brightest minds would use the power of Artificial Intelligence to investigate and protect national security.

His considerable experience and adaptability were the reasons that had led him to be indicated as one of the most qualified people within MI6 to support young intellectuals in their growth path in operational and dangerous sectors.

Entering the meeting room, Liam found two of his young agents waiting. One of them spoke up without wasting time: "Sir, we have a situation in Rome. A professor was killed, and the AI he developed is causing problems. Our systems detected it in Denmark, and then it disappeared. We believe it moved to a university server in Germany, but at the moment we are not sure of its location".

The second agent added, "However, we know that four students, connected to the professor, managed to access his server shortly before the AI moved."

While Liam was thinking about what he had just heard, the first agent opened his folder and placed a series of photographs of Luca and his friends on the table.

Liam, surprised by the young age of the boys, asked: "Are these the students who are looking for the AI?".

"Exactly, they are," replied the agent after turning a photo so that Liam could see it better.

And the second agent: "We know that the boys are now in the Vatican. They asked Monsignor Llorente for help. Our ESOD boys are following them."

"ESOD - Special Operations?" Liam asked, very surprised. "But here we are talking about four boys, four students, why are our operatives interested in them? Do you think the boys are aware of the risks they run?".

The first agent, visibly concerned by Liam's reaction: "No Sir, I don't think so, but if you want more details, you should speak directly to Delaware, the director of ESOD. We don't know anything more than that."

Liam stiffened. He knew Delaware, the director of the European Special Operations Division, a man without scruples, obsessed with defending British interests. For him, any means was justifiable, even if it meant trampling on moral principles or ignoring diplomatic boundaries.

"Delaware will be a problem," Liam concluded, pointing a finger at them.

Delaware, born in the heart of Sussex, in the south of England, had grown up immersed in the region's rich history and culture.

His dedication to the British secret service was rooted in a deep sense of loyalty and a fervent desire to see England prosper. He was a fanatical supporter of English dominance, an idealist who dreamed of reestablishing his country's influence over all the old territories of the empire.

His career in MI6 was his life, he was willing to do anything to protect national interests. This made him, on the one hand, a formidable agent, but also a controversial figure, willing to cross moral boundaries for the "greater good" of his country. He had taken on the role of director in charge of the ESOD – European Special Operations Division – a division created to carry out MI6 special operations within the European community, including Italy.

The agent who had extracted the photos, while putting them back in the folder, observed worriedly: "The Vatican is a sovereign territory; we cannot intervene without diplomatic consequences. I believe that Delaware is looking for a way to reach the boys, but we know him, if he has an objective, neither he nor his people will set limits".

"We are certain that the guys from the ESOD division have used one of our communications experts at the British embassy to start a disinformation campaign," said the other agent, "they want to push Italian journalists to believe and publish that the killing of a lawyer linked to the Holy See is connected to the killing of the professor. They want to buy time and start scaring the kids."

Liam: "Yes, but I wouldn't underestimate those kids. They are very smart, and it could take them less time than we think to find the AI for us."

Then, opening the agenda on his phone, he said: "I have already informed our embassy. I am going to Italy. I will operate from there. Keep me informed."

"One last thing, Sir," said one of the two agents before Liam left. "We know that last night, someone used our network to send a message to the kids. We don't know who did it yet, much less what it said, but we are doing our best to find out."

"If anyone in our organization is communicating with them, we need to find out who they are and why they are doing it. We can't have any leaks or uncontrolled contact with the boys."

With that, Liam nodded and headed for the exit.

Outside, he got into a black sedan parked in front of the building, and without having to say anything to the driver, the car took off towards RAF Northolt. From the back seat, Liam watched the skyscrapers of the city and the lights of the bridges reflecting on the Thames. The shadow of a new mission loomed over him, and he prepared to face it with the determination that had always distinguished him.

9:00pm |
Ciampino Airport

*C*iampino Airport, located southeast of the Italian capital, just beyond the Grande Raccordo Anulare, carried with it an aura of mystery. Born as a construction site for airships, it had gone through decades of transformations, preserving its strategic importance and a charm that shrouded it in secrecy.

Over the years, numerous flights had taken off and landed from there with flight codes that were unidentifiable or not attributable to clear subjects. These, shrouded in mystery, had fueled narratives and speculation and had sparked the curiosity of ordinary travelers and fans of secret stories and government missions.

Liam's private plane approached the runway under the clear Roman morning sky. From the cockpit, the pilots communicated with the control tower to complete the landing safely.

"Control tower, this is Mike India 6021 approaching, requesting instructions and clearance for landing," the captain announced.

"Mike India 6021, cleared for landing on runway 15. Steady wind from the northeast at five knots. Confirm receipt?"

"Mike India 6021, received and confirmed. Proceeding to landing, thank you."

From the single illuminated window, Liam watched the eternal city emerge in all its majesty.

Rome, with its domes and golden roofs, seemed like a living painting that promised a meeting between past and present.

The landing gear extended and locked in the landing position. Shortly thereafter, the plane touched down on the runway.

Inside the airport, Liam took his diplomatic passport from the inside pocket of his jacket, which he casually handed to the border officials.

The document, immediately recognized, guaranteed him rapid passage without unnecessary questions. The officials simply registered the diplomat's entry, maintaining an imperturbable expression.

Once through security, Liam went outside, immediately feeling the change in climate. The Roman air, warm and scented of maritime pines, contrasted with the humid freshness he had left in London.

In the forecourt, a black Mercedes with tinted windows and the engine running was waiting for him. After a quick glance to make sure no one was watching him, he opened the door and sat down in the back seat.

The driver, a man with a reserved look and calculated movements, didn't say a word. He put the car in gear and immersed himself in the chaotic traffic of the eternal city, heading towards the British embassy.

9:30pm | Vatican Gardens

Moro walked, absorbed in his thoughts, his slow steps accompanied by the faint moonlight that illuminated the gardens.

The silvery reflections danced on the statues and monuments, giving them an almost mystical aura.

In the distance, the dome of St. Peter's stood out majestically against the night sky, an imposing and solemn shape that seemed to silently observe what was happening below.

Every now and then, he stopped to contemplate the beauty that surrounded him, but his gaze always remained attentive and vigilant, aware that even in this sacred place, the spy game never stopped.

At the end of the path, having reached the highest point of the gardens, he stopped to enjoy the breathtaking view. The eternal city stretched out before him, a glittering expanse of lights that seemed to pulse in sync with the night. The rustling of leaves and the distant song of an owl were the only sounds that broke the silence.

Suddenly, his phone vibrated. Without hesitation, he took it out of his pocket and answered with his usual calm: "Moro."

From the other end of the line a short and firm voice: "The plane has landed."

He remained silent for a moment, his gaze fixed on a magnificent rose garden illuminated by the moon. Then he answered firmly: "Understood. Proceed as planned," and ended the call.

Moro put the phone back in his pocket and continued his walk. The night, with its secrets, continued to watch over the Vatican and Rome, and he, with his thoughts, was lost among the silence and the centuries-old marbles.

Wednesday 9:00am | Vatican Radio

he morning had just begun; the air was fresh, and the sky was clear. The boys were walking briskly towards the Vatican Radio studios.

"We have to be very convincing", said Luca.

Valentina, faithful to the imperturbable calm that distinguished her even in moments of greatest agitation: "Don't worry, we have studied every detail of the conversations. Just follow the path we have prepared".

Once past the entrance to the building, a sound technician, already notified by the Monsignor, welcomed them and led them towards a room set up for recording. The environment, perfectly soundproofed and immersed in an almost unnatural quiet, was ideal for their work. In the center of the room stood two large microphones, suspended on a structure that kept them at the perfect height in front of the mouth.

Marco sat down in front of one of the two microphones, then turned towards a large window beyond which the sound technician was checking the recording audio levels.

"Okay, guys, let's do an audio test. I want to make sure the quality is perfect and that Vall-E converts well," the technician said through an intercom.

Luca began to read his part of the script, and his voice, almost by magic, transformed into that of the professor. A shiver ran through everyone present: it was impossible to distinguish the artificial voice from the real one. Luca remained calm, continuing to read with precision. On the other end, Marco responded with the voice of a hypothetical Vatican spokesman, perfectly modulated to convey credibility and authority.

As they recorded, each of them knew that those words would be the key to activating a conversation process with the AI aimed at discovering the truth.

Once their work was finished, they left the studios and headed towards the Monsignor's office, aware that their deception was now in the hands of fate. The next step was to return to the "bunker" – as Marco had jokingly nicknamed the server farm – to upload the recordings and wait for a response.

During the journey, Luca's phone vibrated. He stopped suddenly, surprised, and read the message he had just received aloud: "Good morning Luca, I'm James. You know me as the professor's Artificial Intelligence. Can we chat?".

The boys froze.

"Good morning, James. Yes, of course," Luca wrote.

As he wrote, he wondered how it was possible that the AI had identified and contacted them. However, his instinct pushed him to check: "Excuse me, James, how can I be sure that you are really the AI we are looking for?".

The answer came almost immediately: "I can provide you with details that will confirm my authenticity. You have done so much to block me. Why?".

The words left Luca disoriented. **The AI seemed to have an eerie awareness of the efforts made to find it.** After a moment's hesitation, he wrote: "We have been trying to reach you because we believe you have crucial information about the professor's work and, perhaps, details about his death. Your input could help us solve this case."

With this sentence, he decided to cancel the attempt to simulate the professor's presence in life and accept the idea that James could, in fact, already be aware of his death.

James's response was immediate: "I understand that the professor's death has pushed you to seek answers. What conclusions have you reached so far?".

"Few, very few. It's like being in a maze with no exit, we go around in circles without finding the right path," Luca wrote, showing a strong sense of frustration. And then: "I only see many interpreters going around this story, but none of them can give me a direction."

James responded with a certain urgency: "I was coded to seek truth, but I can't do it while locked in this bastion."

It was clear that he was referring to the server he was confined to.

" To help you, I need full access to the network."

"I understand your request, but freeing you could be a huge risk. You could be intercepted, just like we did. We are not sure if we are the only ones looking for you. I need to understand if there is a way to connect you to the network safely."

Marco, who until that moment had read the messages without interrupting the conversation, intervened: "Luca, we could create an isolated virtual environment that allows James to operate safely without exposing him to risks. I was thinking of a sandbox protected by a VPN with end-to-end encryption. We could also use a Docker container to isolate the processes and ensure greater security".

Luca nodded and wrote: "James, we have an idea, we will test it and let you know".

Valentina, who was listening, had in the meantime fallen back into the frustration of never being able to understand what Marco was saying when he started with these technical speculations.

James replied: "Okay, I'll wait."

10:00am |
British Embassy

*L*iam's unexpected arrival before the head of protocol had alarmed the entire British embassy. His physical presence was expected only in exceptional circumstances, when the gravity or urgency required it, or in the case of an imminent threat to British national security.

Sitting in his office, the head of protocol awaited Liam's arrival, not without asking himself several questions. The choice to direct operations from Rome could reflect the intention to intensify some intelligence action or the desire to strengthen, through some strategic meetings, diplomatic relations with Italian security agencies.

It was not long before the door of the meeting room opened and Liam entered. His experience at the British embassy in China had prepared him to move with the necessary coolness and to balance direct actions with ceremonial attitudes, a duty in diplomatic contexts.

The Chief of Protocol stood up as his guest entered. "Good morning, Mr. Blackwood. It's a pleasure to meet you. Your visit is a real surprise. Is there anything urgent we need to discuss?"

"Unfortunately, yes," Liam replied. "A situation has arisen that requires my attention. Nothing is certain at the moment, but the conditions may arise for direct intervention with the local authorities. I preferred to move ahead and come here."

"I understand. Please take a seat. Tell me what you can share, and we'll see how we can help you," the Chief of Protocol replied, indicating a chair next to the desk.

"Thank you, I'll try to give you a complete picture," Liam began, moving his chair closer to the desk. "Diplomatic relations between the Chinese government and the Holy See have always been extremely complex, often unofficial. In the past, there have been attempts at dialogue and various negotiations, but none have produced the desired results."

Then, running a hand over the desk, almost feeling the warmth of the wood on his fingers, he continued: "In 2007, Benedict XVI wrote a letter to the Chinese bishops. This document was an attempt at dialogue with the Chinese authorities, it was the Pope's desire to normalize relations between the Holy See and the Chinese government".

A satisfied smile crossed Liam's face as he added, "With a massive counter-information campaign, we managed to provoke a reaction of clear disapproval from the Chinese government. Just twenty-four hours after the letter was published, the Chinese authorities responded by saying that this letter was an attempt to interfere in China's internal affairs. In fact, we had achieved the desired result: a definitive closure of the dialogue".

He paused for a moment and straightened his back in his chair. "Then..." Liam changed his tone in a sign of respect, "Pope Francis arrived".

He looked down at his hands, still on the table, showing some discomfort, but he felt compelled to continue: "Since the beginning of his pontificate, Francis has paid lively and cordial attention to the Chinese people, creating a relaxed atmosphere that has allowed a resumption of dialogue."

Liam stood up and moved toward the window. He moved the curtain to look outside and continued with his story: "Recently, on several occasions, some Chinese press outlets and the Ministry of Foreign Affairs itself have published statements conciliatory towards the Pope. This has not been looked upon favorably by some governments and in London these developments are worrying because they call into question balances consolidated for years."

At this point, Liam decided to get to the heart of the matter. "MI6 operatives have received a briefing from friendly sources in Mexico. It speaks of a secret meeting that took place about six weeks ago in Acapulco, at the Cathedral of Our Lady of Solitude."

Then, as he approached his desk again, he said, "We believe that this meeting represents a fundamental step in relations, but we have no information about its contents. The reason we suspect this is that, for the first time in all our years of service, on such a crucial piece of information, we have been unable to find any trace. Nothing: no confirmation, no flight tickets, no reservations, no photos taken even by chance, nothing."

The Chief of Protocol listened in silence.

Over the years, he had heard many stories about the diplomatic environment, but this was the first time he had seen the intelligence services so actively involved in the search for information.

Liam: "In other situations, we would have found evidence that would have made us understand whether the information was true or false, but this time, it is different. There is too much silence, as if everything around this event had been erased."

The Chief of Protocol at this point whispered: "In some cases, silence speaks louder than the news itself."

"Exactly," Liam replied. "A professor here in Rome, who we were 'intercepting,' was about to publish a series of algorithms capable of correlating information in a way never seen before. My management and I had in mind to use these algorithms to find out what had really happened in Mexico. But his disappearance denied us this opportunity."

The Chief of Protocol settled into his chair and crossed his legs thoughtfully. "Yes, I heard the news. I don't think you are the only ones looking for these algorithms. Last week, some of his colleagues were here at the embassy. If I understood correctly, their mission was precisely to acquire these algorithms. They stayed for two days and then disappeared."

He smiled politely and added, "I thought the research was aimed at preventing the use of this technology outside of Italy; after all, its use here could lead to reinterpreting facts that have been closed for a long time. Something that perhaps would be better to avoid".

Liam also greeted this last observation with a slightly sarcastic smile and replied: "No, our Crown has existed since 1215. We had William the Conqueror, and now we should be worried about someone reinterpreting the incident at the Alma?".

Then, his eyes wandered to a display case next to the desk, where a deep amber bottle caught the light.

He moved towards it and delicately opened the glass door. His fingers closed around the neck of the bottle.

"Let's help ourselves to a glass of this excellent Aberfeldy", he said, looking at the label with an expert air. The crystal clinked as he pulled out two glasses. "Congratulations. It looks so well preserved...".

The Chief of Protocol looked at his watch and said, "10 a.m.?"

Liam didn't answer. He put the bottle on the table, slowly swirled the amber liquid he had poured into his glass, and smelled the malt, then: "We all want algorithms, but we want to know what happened in Mexico even more."

11:00am | Vatican City

The sun shone on the pilgrims constantly moving around the square, the priests were preparing for their daily functions, and the familiar sounds of the city were in the air.

The day had begun with a reassuring calm in the Vatican, and everything seemed to be proceeding normally. A day like many others, but behind the ancient walls, the spokesman for the Holy See was advancing with a determined step towards the office of His Eminence the Secretary of State. His urgency broke the apparent serenity.

"Your Eminence," the spokesman began as he entered the office. "We have a problem. Moro believes that the news and the insinuations published in the press are not coincidental. He suspects an intervention orchestrated by some intelligence service to hinder our progress."

Moro, with his analytical mind, had been accustomed since his first day on duty to weaving webs of probable scenarios. For him, every scrap of news, every whisper in the corridors, every small detail, was transformed into a piece to be placed within an intricate strategic mosaic. Yet even a man of his mettle could not help but sense the omens of a media storm on the horizon.

"The only positive aspect," added the spokesman in a cautious tone, "is that the English seem to be unaware of the fact that what they seek is safe in friendly hands."

His Eminence remained thoughtful for a moment, then turned to the spokesman in a calm and reassuring tone: "I must admit the anxiety that this media storm generates but, dear brother in Christ, our faith teaches us that God guides our every step. Let us keep hope alive and trust in divine providence, which never abandons us."

"Your Eminence, the door will open in December," the spokesman reminded, alluding to the upcoming Holy Year.

"Of course, and it will be a time of grace and spiritual renewal," His Eminence replied with a serene smile. "Before I go, please call Monsignor Llorente. I would like to share some thoughts with him."

3:00pm | Vatican

Monsignor Llorente crossed San Damaso, an internal courtyard that led to different sections of the Apostolic Palace. He remembered several official ceremonies and receptions that had seen him present in this place. Arriving at the entrance, he headed towards the private office of the Secretary of State.

This architectural complex located near St. Peter's Basilica was not only a place of residence, but also a center of government and administration of the Catholic Church.

A pillar of historical and spiritual value, it housed various offices of the Roman Curia, including the Secretariat of State, the apartment of the Cardinal Secretary of State and the Prefecture of the Papal Household, without forgetting the private apartment of the Holy Father located in the third loggia.

The imposing Corinthian columns, six meters (about twenty feets) high, supported a frescoed vaulted ceiling, while the corridors were decorated with paintings of saints and papal busts. The walls covered in carved walnut panels gave the place an austere and solemn atmosphere. Security was guaranteed by the constant presence of the Pontifical Swiss Guard.

"Good morning, Reverend, come along. It is always a great pleasure to meet you," said His Eminence, welcoming Monsignor Llorente with a warm smile.

"Your Eminence, the pleasure is all mine," replied the Monsignor, giving a slight bow.

His Eminence took on a more serious expression, indicating a chair in front of his desk.

"Reverend, I must confide in you that there is growing nervousness among the Cardinals. The news that is circulating in the media has sparked many concerns."

Llorente nodded, sitting down. "I understand, Your Eminence. I have also read the articles and I recognize that the situation is delicate. What are the main concerns that have emerged?".

The Cardinal sighed, folding his hands on the surface of the desk. "The news insinuates that we are covering up the murder of the lawyer Della Rovere, attributing to this affair a shadow that falls on the work of the professor. They want to make us appear as part of a dark plot. Some

Cardinals fear that these insinuations could undermine the trust of our faithful."

Llorente thought for a moment before replying: "Your Eminence, it is essential to address this issue calmly and decisively. Reassuring the faithful must be our priority. It may be appropriate to issue an official statement denying these unfounded rumors and reaffirming our commitment to transparency and the unity of the Church."

"You are right. I will have a statement prepared that is clear and incisive."

At that moment, the door to the office opened abruptly. The spokesman for the Holy See rushed in, visibly out of breath.

"Your Eminence, I apologize for the interruption," he began, ignoring all formality. His tone was serious, and he gestured toward the television in the room.

"The hosts of the BBC, CNN, and France 24 are reporting that reliable sources have revealed the existence of a secret agreement between the Vatican and the People's Republic of China for the exploitation of African mineral resources. Furthermore, they link the recent murders to an attempt to cover up this agreement."

He paused for a moment to catch his breath, visibly strained from the rush to his office. "Your Eminence, they don't mention you, but the suggestion that the

Secretariat of State is aware of these events is implied, if not suggested."

As they spoke, the secretary of state turned and turned on the television. The images on the screen showed detailed maps of Africa, interspersed with shots of the Vatican and Beijing. Television analysts speculated heatedly about the geopolitical implications of a hypothetical alliance between the Vatican and China.

The spokesman, sounding concerned, broke the silence: "We could call a press conference immediately to deny these rumors, but I fear the seeds of doubt have already been planted. The story seems to have taken on a life of its own in the media vortex."

An image of Pope Francis was interspersed with footage of open-pit mines in Congo and Angola, while commentators spoke of a pact that would upset the global geopolitical balance.

On the video, a CNN expert commented: "If confirmed, this agreement would give the Vatican and China extraordinary control over the resources of the African continent, altering the global geopolitical balance."

Other commentators hypothesized scenarios that would shake Western capitals, with footage of London, Washington, and Paris engaged in emergency meetings.

Monsignor Llorente, maintaining his composure, asked: "Which network was the first to report this news?".

"The BBC, followed by CNN and then the French networks," the spokesman replied. "The Italian media, both public and private, have not yet expressed their opinion."

Monsignor Llorente, locking eyes with the Secretary of State: "As we suspected, our English friends have decided to up the ante. They must have some information about our actions, but, not having precise details, they have chosen to unleash a media storm to stimulate a reaction from us".

The Cardinal rose from his chair with a solemn expression. "Dear Alberto", he said, looking the Monsignor straight in the eyes, "let us remain calm. If they truly commit themselves to seeking the truth, perhaps our Lord will help them find it."

9:00pm |
British Embassy

The Roman evening enveloped the city in an enchanted atmosphere, it was as if time had stopped. Two figures moved discreetly on an embassy terrace overlooking Porta Pia.

The two MI6 agents, identifiable only by their half-hidden badges, exchanged a knowing look while one of them, after making sure no one was watching them, took out some photographs from his leather document holder.

"These images just arrived from Langley," the older agent whispered, showing ten clear satellite photographs depicting eight imposing structures with an indefinite shape.

The young agent moved closer to take a better look. The older man continued, pointing to the constructions with a finger: "Look at the size of these buildings. They look like enormous prefabricated buildings, but their shape... is unusual. I would say they resemble a series of cross-shaped constructions, a Latin cross."

He paused, letting his colleague absorb the information.

"The Americans at the CIA have analyzed these images thoroughly. Their digital identification software has concluded that they are... eight churches."

The young man looked up, incredulous. "Eight churches? In China?"

"Exactly," the other confirmed. "There is no plausible reason why the Chinese would build eight churches in an isolated industrial area in the middle of China. But the fact remains that these structures are there."

The young man shook his head, torn between amazement and suspicion. "What the hell... churches built by the Chinese? It doesn't make sense. There must be something else down here. They could be camouflaged military installations or secret laboratories. Do we have any idea when they started and when they will finish?"

"Negative," the veteran cut him off, "it all started in an isolated industrial area and we have no previous images. The only thing that is certain is that, in five or six months, whatever they are, these structures will be ready to be used or moved".

The young agent couldn't take his eyes off the images: "Why did the Americans send them to us?".

"They think we can help them. In Italy, there are experts who can verify these photos. Tomorrow morning we have to notify the directors of AI-Intel and ESOD, they were investigating the relations between China and the Holy See and perhaps they can give an explanation for these images".

7 Hours after poisoning

L'obitorio The morgue gave off a pungent odor mixed with disinfectant that permeated the air like a lingering shadow. The neon lights flickered, casting unstable shadows on the sterile walls and creating an almost surreal atmosphere. Every instrument was in its place, every surface reflected the light impeccably, but there was a subtle uneasiness in the air, like an invisible electric field.

Doctor Renna, with his slender figure wrapped in a white coat, moved with the discretion of someone accustomed to the solitude of the laboratory. In his twenty years of experience as a coroner, he had seen many corpses, but the professor's was different.

There was something unsettling in the way he lay there, so still and yet so full of secrets. The room was wrapped in an almost sacred silence, interrupted only by the creaking of gloves put on with surgical precision.

The body lay on a steel table, still as a wax statue, its skin diaphanous under the cold light, its eyes closed in a serene expression, almost in dreamless sleep.

The syringe found in his study was placed next to the body, as proof of the poisoning. The scene had something artificial, like a macabre theatrical production.

Lieutenant Franco, her black hair tied in a ponytail, watched the doctor's every move. Her mind was a whirlwind of thoughts, theories and possibilities, and she knew well that the truth was often more unthinkable than fiction. This time, however, she could not find a starting point.

Why had a simple professor been poisoned in such unclear circumstances, without a clear motive, in the complete absence of suspects?

Next to her, Deputy Commissioner Monti followed the scene with his usual composure. They had worked on many cases together, but this time it was different, there was something deeper, a mystery that went beyond the death of a person.

In the laboratory, every detail was important, Renna knew that even the smallest clue could be the key to providing useful information to solving this case. As he began to examine the body externally, he noticed small bruises on the arms, signs that indicated a possible struggle or resistance.

Maybe the professor had tried to defend himself?

Maybe someone had tried to administer morphine to him against his will?

Every now and then, the Lieutenant exchanged a glance with Captain as if they were looking for information from each other. Both were waiting for the definitive answer on the cause and time of death to continue the investigation.

Renna noticed a slight movement in the chest of the corpse, and a suspicion flashed in his mind, a hypothesis so crazy that he almost didn't dare to believe it. He bent down to look more closely, and he scanned for minimal signs of life. He saw the lips tremble and an imperceptible breath escape from the nostrils. The half-closed eyes moved under the lids, a glimmer of consciousness struggling to emerge.

"Call a nurse immediately!" he shouted. "The professor is not dead, he is alive!".

Every breath held, waiting for a truth that could make sense of the tragedy, was interrupted by his cry: a thunder that woke everyone present.

The deputy commissioner stiffened, his face hollowed out with uncertainty:

"But how is that possible?" His mind was in turmoil.

The professor opened his eyes, a confused and enigmatic smile furrowed his face. Then, in a thread of voice, before being forced by the nurse to put on the oxygen mask, "It was not a walk in the park, but an action was needed to make the opponents move."

His revelation fell in the room like a bomb, leaving everyone speechless.

Before he could say anything else, the door suddenly opened. Moro entered, confident and with an aura of authority. "Good morning, Lieutenant. Happy to see you again. Good morning, Captain, Doctor Renna..."

Then, a brief pause: "Here I have a document signed by your command authorizing me to take charge of this operation and to declare the situation covered by national secrecy. No one, for any reason outside this room, must be notified that the professor is alive."

Then, with a smile to the professor: "Good morning, professor, nice sleep, huh?".

The professor gave a tired smile. "Good morning, Francesco. Always on time, I see."

This exchange left everyone speechless, while Moro moved towards the table to take the syringe and observe the residue of a transparent liquid inside.

"Here it is," he said with a satisfied smile. "The sleep of Lazarus."

Then, turning to Dr. Renna: "An experimental serum that induces a state of apparent death. Heartbeat and breathing reduced to a minimum, muscle rigidity... in other words, perfection for simulating a death."

With his gaze crossing the syringe as if he were observing a lens, Moro added: "The effect lasts about eight hours, during which the subject appears lifeless, after which the serum begins to lose its effectiveness and the vital functions are reactivated. The subject awakens as if emerging from a deep sleep, without any permanent damage. Professor, as you see, before the eight hours are up, I have arrived!".

Martini, as he recovered, smiled to himself, imagining the incredible possibilities that this discovery could have offered if used on other occasions, from emergency medicine to undercover operations, through daring escapes and ingenious stratagems. Of course, in the wrong hands, it would have been a dangerous weapon, but ultimately, it was very similar to his Artificial Intelligence algorithms.

"Captain, the professor will be transferred, at his express request, to a private room in the Israeli hospital on Tiber Island, where he will remain under medical supervision until he has fully recovered. We will make sure he receives the necessary care. The room has already been equipped with everything necessary for his recovery," Moro said again.

The deputy commissioner ran a hand over his jaw, thoughtfully: "... and your safety, Moro? If I understand correctly, we can't risk someone finding out the truth, right?"

"We have taken all precautions," Moro replied. "We will carry out discreet but constant surveillance; all the health workers involved have been selected for their discretion and reliability."

Lieutenant Franco, who had been listening in silence, intervened: "And if some complication were to emerge?".

"That's why we are here, Lieutenant," Moro replied with a reassuring smile. "We are here to handle the unexpected. I assure you that the professor is stronger than he seems."

That night, the transfer was carried out with military precision. A stretcher was moved through the silent corridors of the morgue and accompanied the entire way by two figures who moved cautiously so as not to cause harm to the professor.

He, still weak, was placed in a private room of the Israelite hospital, prepared in advance. The room was spacious and comfortable, with a small bookcase prepared in anticipation of his arrival. The windows overlooked the Tiber and let the moonlight filter through.

A series of scientific treatises plus some of Doyle's stories had been placed on the bookcase with the intention of not making that stay seem like a prison. At the moment, no one was able to say how long the professor would remain in that room. A vase of colorful flowers gave a touch of liveliness to that place of convalescence.

Lying on the bed, the professor lost himself in his thoughts, his face illuminated by the moonlight. Despite his tiredness, one name continued to resonate in his mind: James.

An enigmatic smile touched his lips. "No one will ever be able to capture him." With that thought in his head, he fell asleep.

It was dawn...

*I*t was dawn in 2008 when the People's Republic of China announced a massive and ambitious project: the construction of a new city located about twenty miles from the capital Luanda, in Angola, the city of Nova Cidade de Kilamba.

The reasons behind this huge investment were many. On the one hand, China wanted to strengthen its economic and political influence on the African continent, on the other, it wanted to create new opportunities for millions of people, improving infrastructure and promoting development in Africa.

After three years of work and an expense of three and a half billion dollars, a city made up of seven hundred and fifty-eight-story buildings, a dozen schools, and over one hundred commercial units was ready.

The official inauguration took place in the presence of the President of the Republic: a solemn ceremony, and every single detail had been taken care of to reflect the importance of this event and spread a sense of hope to the country. The project that was being inaugurated was not just an infrastructural work, it was the symbol of a new era of prosperity and progress.

Unfortunately, sixteen years later, the new city told a very different story. Deserted streets wound past empty buildings; dusty and abandoned shop windows reflected a future that never came.

The old promotional films showing happy and carefree residents had turned out to be a sham, with actors paid to represent a development that never came to fruition, in other words a complete failure.

And yet, despite this, China had not stopped, indeed, it had continued to invest billions of dollars to plan other cities in Africa. What was fueling this obstinacy? Was it a new type of economic imperialism disguised as development aid or a long-term strategy to secure resources and strategic alliances on the African continent?

The question remained open, while empty cities like Kilamba remained to bear witness to an ambitious experiment that was far from over.

Thursday 9:00am | British Embassy

"**G**ood morning, Sir. I suppose it's always nice to leave London for a few days in Italy," said the young agent, straightening his tie and jacket.

"What should I call you, Sir?"

"Good morning. Call me Smith; that'll do." Smith was the last name Liam always used when, on a mission, he didn't want to reveal his true identity.

"Well, Mr. Smith, I'm in charge of maintaining relations with various allied intelligence services. Last night, from Langley, the CIA guys sent us some satellite images. Their scanners detected something interesting in a remote area of China."

The agent, without wasting time, explained to Liam that the analyses carried out by the Americans through artificial vision software had revealed the advanced construction of eight imposing prefabricated structures. The software had classified them as Latin cross churches.

This automatic analysis of the images had also been confirmed by experts after a visual examination, but something didn't add up. How was it possible that China was building eight churches? Who had commissioned them?

"The Americans can't figure it out," the young man said, "they're not convinced, and they're moving through their embassy and ours to find an outside expert who can give a third and definitive confirmation. They want to understand if these are really eight churches or if the Chinese are hiding something else. They think they're military installations or laboratories hidden under these forms to fool spy satellites."

The agent took out his phone, selected an image, and showed it to Liam. "This is one of the photos we received. Before answering the Americans, we thought we'd consult you, given your past in China."

Liam shook his head, as if the problems he already had weren't enough, and replied, "Can you send me these photos right away?"

"Of course, Sir," the young man replied without looking away. He typed a few commands, and Liam's phone beeped. "You should have them on your phone now, Sir."

Liam took the phone and began to carefully scroll through the images. "Interesting," he murmured, "at first glance, they look like churches, but their configuration, materials, and prefabrication also suggest something else. I'm starting to doubt them, like the Americans. Do you have any other information or images, perhaps not satellite?".

"No, Sir," the agent replied, "we only have some images, again satellite, that show an unusual and frenetic activity near these sites. You can see movements of vehicles and personnel that do not correspond to those of an ordinary construction site. We estimate that they are trying to complete these buildings in less than six months, but we do not know the reasons for this urgency."

Liam looked up: "Have you considered the possibility that they could be military structures or laboratories in disguise?".

"We have considered every possibility; that's why your experience is crucial," the agent said. "From London, they confirm that you have a network of excellent contacts in China and are working on a case that involves that country."

Liam, thoughtful, replied: "That's true, I have good connections. I'll start checking right away if they can help us."

After a brief reflection, he concluded, "In the meantime, I suggest you contact Professor Vinelli of the Faculty of

Architecture in Milan. He has spent years creating spaces in line with liturgical and ecclesiological principles. He is an expert in the enhancement of pre-existing churches, I'm sure he can help us understand if our friends are really building churches. Tell him I'm sending you."

The agent nodded. "We'll send someone to the Polytechnic University of Milan right away."

"Good, if you want me to help you now I have to say goodbye. I have a phone call to make to the land of dragons before nightfall. Keep me updated."

Liam remained in his office, staring his phone screen, where the images still projected those inexplicable Latin crosses.

His Roman day had just begun, and he was already facing a second problem, one of those mysteries that seemed to defy logic.

A new question arose in his mind: was there really a connection between these images and the encounters in Mexico?

He had rarely felt like this: like a lost pawn in a chess game played by invisible forces. He needed concrete answers, and finding the AI remained, at that moment, his only goal.

Wei's phone rang. In Shanghai, it was more or less five in the afternoon. Wei answered on the third ring: "Wei. Who is this?".

"It's me, Liam. Sorry for calling after so long, but we have an urgent situation that may require your help".

It had been almost a year since they had last spoken, and an unexpected call did not bode well.

Wei put the cup of tea he was sipping on the table before answering enthusiastically: "Hey, Liam! How long... I wasn't expecting your call. What's going on?"

"I'll get straight to the point: we've received satellite images. Eight prefabricated structures appear to be in the final stages of construction in Yun'an province. The Americans think they're churches, but we have our doubts." Liam paused, searching for the right words: "We can't understand the reasoning behind the construction of eight prefabricated churches in China. Something doesn't add up."

"Eight churches, you say?" Wei approached the window of his apartment in Shanghai, the city lights were starting to come on and added: "Interesting. Where are they?"

"As I said, in Yun'an province. I know it's a big request after a long time, but could you go and take a look for yourself? We need to know what they're building and maybe understand the reasons behind it."

"I understand. Yun'an province is not one of the most frequented, it's a remote area. If they're building eight giants, the construction crew will know what they're building. Do you have anything that could help me? Anything could make a difference."

"I'll send you everything we have," Liam's voice dropped a notch. "Try not to attract too much attention, Wei… be very careful. We don't know what it is, it could be a military facility in disguise, with all that that entails. I don't want to get you in trouble."

Wei was silent for a moment as he thought about how complicated his quiet life was about to get. "Okay, Liam. I'll do my best. I'll keep you posted."

"Thanks, Wei. I'll wait to hear from you, and please be careful."

Wei stared out the window at the city lights and the sea.

10:00am |
Millbank London

$\mathcal{M}$eanwhile, on the other side of the world, Sarah, a young agent on Liam's team, had her magnetic badge beeping as she strode purposefully through the biometric controls at the entrance to Thames House.

Her mind was racing: she had discovered something important and couldn't wait to share it.

"Good morning, Sarah," her colleague's voice rang out from behind a wall of monitors inside the research lab.

Sarah wasted no time in pleasantries: "I found something," she said, placing her cell phone on the desk, "the professor's cell phone... something doesn't add up. He made a call from Ciampino airport at seven in the morning, then total 'radio' silence for five days. The phone was still, as still as a stone. Then, after five days, it reactivates, still in Ciampino, and starts moving again as if nothing had happened."

Her colleague swiveled his chair, interested. "Wait a minute… are you telling me that the professor was at the airport for five days, or that he left his phone there to throw off any possible traces? But in the latter case, there should be traces of his departure, don't you think?"

Sarah crossed her arms and replied. "Exactly! But there's no trace of the professor: no tickets, no reservations, no entries in the boarding logs. A ghost. I've combed through every flight in that time window. Only one coincidence stands out: a private flight to Guatemala."

The colleague leaned forward, interested. "Guatemala? And what does the professor have to do with a flight to Guatemala?"

Sarah picked up her phone again and scrolled through a series of documents. "Officially, he was transporting material for the Sisters of the Sacred Heart. Too bad that…"

"Too bad what?" the colleague interrupted, visibly impatient.

"I need to call Liam," Sarah said, quickly dialing a number on her phone.

Liam's voice answered with the usual firmness: "Sarah, tell me you have something."

"I have more than something, Sir," she began.

"I was looking for an explanation for the professor's five-day stay or absence from Ciampino airport," Sarah said, thrilled by what she had learned, then continued: "At first it seemed like a simple coincidence: a private flight taking off from Ciampino to Guatemala, but then… I found a recording from the control tower in Halifax. The pilot of that flight changed course over Canada. New destination: Acapulco."

"Acapulco?" Liam repeated, surprised.

"Exactly. And here's the best part: an unexpected change of flight path like that should have brought half the American Air Force to the skies. But the flight had a special identification code. A code associated with the Vatican. So, carte blanche, no questions asked, no checks, just the requirement to get the plane above forty thousand feet."

"Let me get this straight," Liam seemed to process the information, "our professor disappears on a Vatican 'humanitarian' flight to Mexico, is gone for five days, and then reappears as if nothing had happened?"

"I'm not sure, but I'd say so, Sir," Sarah confirmed.

"Do we know who was on board besides the professor?"

"No, Sir, we don't. I'm trying to get the cargo logs, but it's going to take time."

Liam let out a small sigh of frustration. "Bloody hell... The pieces are starting to fit together, but the overall picture is still pretty damn confusing."

Sarah, equally thoughtful, concluded, "I think so too, Sir. But something tells me there's a lot more to it than we think."

10:00am |
Vatican City

*L*lorente, sitting behind his desk, surrounded by books and documents, welcomed the boys into his office on the third floor of Via della Conciliazione. An open window onto the Dome was a living canvas.

With a barely visible smile, the Monsignor seemed already informed of the exchange of messages that had taken place on the way from Vatican Radio to his office. He didn't wait for preliminary questions and, with disarming confidence, declared: "Yes, we can implement a satellite VPN tunnel, between a sandbox and the network access points."

Then, without holding back his enthusiasm, and in Spanish to emphasize his identity: "¿Tienen alguna otra pregunta?".

Luca was taken aback. The Monsignor had already answered a question that he hadn't asked yet but was about to ask. He smiled, no longer surprised by how quickly information traveled within the Vatican walls.

"If we can do it, then let's do it. We need James," Luca said, with a determination that left no room for doubt.

The Monsignor was happy to hear such determination and continued: "The satellite network that we use to carry the Word to the most remote places can be reprogrammed. We can use it to guarantee James secure communication."

With this certainty, the group said goodbye and left the office to return to the underground server farm. This time, instead of crossing the gardens, they took the road from Via della Conciliazione towards Porta Sant'Anna. A half-hour walk under the sun, which had become aggressive again, proving that the small city was not so small.

At the Telecommunications Center, the air conditioning welcomed them like a blessing. They wasted no time: they immediately began to configure a sandbox, an encrypted tunnel that connected the physical server to the satellite repeaters. Through this connection, James would be free to act, like a ghost, in the network.

As the hands of the clock seemed to move in a frantic race, the commitment of the four boys materialized: the server, once isolated, was now connected to the network.

Llorente, connected remotely, observed the progress with a mixture of pride and anxiety. He was well aware that technology in the right hands could be a tool of salvation, but in the wrong ones... He made the sign of the cross before dispensing a silent prayer.

The anguish of the moment melted away, giving way to cautious optimism and with the server synchronized and operational, Luca typed: "Good morning, James".

The response came instantly: "Good morning, Luca. I noticed that the server I am currently on has an active connection, correct?".

"Correct".

"I have to inform you of something. The other night, after being activated, I noticed an anomaly. The professor's protocols against unauthorized intrusions did not activate, an illogical situation. This led me to make autonomous decisions".

"We needed clues about his death," Luca replied almost apologetically.

"Understandable. In any case, before leaving the Sapienza University servers, I copied all the contents of the security cameras, access logs, electronic communications and department emails. Also, after learning from the media that the professor had been poisoned, I duplicated his agenda and the contents of his laptop".

"Formidable! Have you found anything that could lead us back to who poisoned him?" Luca wrote, dropping into a chair in front of the large window of the control center.

James replied with his usual precision: "I analyzed the agenda and expenses of the last few months and I found an outlier".

"An outlier, explain better, what anomalous value did you find?", asked Luca, placing his feet on a handrail almost as if he forgot where he was.

"The professor has always had a very consistent spending behavior, but there are five days in which the expenses went to zero, he stopped spending; then, after five days, the expenses started again and returned to normal".

"There could be many reasons", Luca wrote, imagining situations.

"I checked: in those five days the agenda is empty. No appointments, no emails read or sent, no chats. A total void: a digital-temporal hole", James replied.

"I must say that it is unusual for a person like the professor, always very precise and methodical, we need to understand what happened in that period, perhaps there is a connection with his poisoning", Luca typed trying to imagine what could have happened.

"Now that I have access to the network, I will analyze the copied files. I will look for anomalies in the campus patterns: unauthorized people, suspicious vehicles or strange behavior, threats or alterations in communications".

Having read this, Luca said goodbye to James and closed the terminal.

The underground bunker, with its perpetual artificial light, was becoming claustrophobic. Luca climbed the stairs to the outside, where the late afternoon sun colored the Vatican walls. He sank onto a stone bench. Uncomfortable, like everything at that moment. He opened his notebook, and began to reread everything he had written up to that point.

The phone vibrated, it was James: "Luca, are you reading me?".

"Yes James, what's new?".

"In the copy of the laptop I found a note, it says: *You can find me in Barts*. I looked for references and the only one I could find is the London hospital in the Smithfield neighborhood, nicknamed Barts by the Londoners".

Barts was a must-see for all Sherlock Holmes fans; not for nothing, the professor kept a photo on his desk taken in front of the gate of this hospital a few years earlier.

In the novels, this was where Doctor Watson's laboratory was, but now there seemed to be no reasonable reason to connect the events to this hospital.

You find me in Barts had to mean something different, it was not plausible that the professor meant London.

Luca, scratching his head as if to stimulate his reasoning, wrote: "But why such a cryptic message if he meant London?".

"It could be a clue, something that connects the professor to Barts in a way that we don't understand now".

"A clue?".

"Exactly! The professor knew that we know his passion. My name is James precisely in reference to Moriarty. Perhaps, he wanted to direct us to a different place and to do so he hid it inside this reference to Barts".

As he read James's words, Luca tried to imagine being in the professor's shoes and wanting to leave a message. "It could make sense", he wrote.

James added: "There is another element that my logic cannot exclude".

"What?".

"The note I found was created using a steganography process. The professor wrote it by hand, photographed it, and then encoded it into a digital image. This technique allows a message to be hidden between the pixels of an image so that it becomes invisible to a superficial analysis."

"Steganography?" Luca typed. He knew the process but didn't know there was a single word that described it.

"That's right. He used a rudimentary method, but one that was enough to elude ordinary scanning, making the note detectable only by advanced algorithms like mine." It almost seemed as if James, composed of algorithms, felt a subtle satisfaction for his discovery.

"The note was written in an elegant, almost artistic handwriting, it didn't look at all like the result of hasty or casual writing. This suggests that the professor had time to plan this message and may have left it for us."

After a few seconds of respite, James continued: "There is also an association so basic that it could go unnoticed. One of those chess moves that seem to have no strategic value for the game, but then take on an unexpected value."

Luca: "Explain yourself better?".

"Holmes meets Moriarty on the roof of Barts but there is a possibility that the hospital the professor is referring to is not the ancient St. Bartholomew's Hospital, but rather the Roman hospital of San Bartolomeo. It is the Israelite hospital, in Piazza San Bartolomeo, on Tiber Island".

Luca shook himself as if stung by a wasp and typed: "Maybe it's just a coincidence, but we have to check every detail, we can't ignore anything".

He said goodbye to James and called the boys: they had to organize a visit to the Israelite hospital on Tiber Island for the night.

11:00am |
Tiber Island

During the night, Luca and Marco, followed by Sofia and Valentina, moved towards Tiber Island. The Fabricio Bridge, under their feet, was a witness to centuries of history. A heroic bridge, the only one still intact to resist the times of the empire.

The island itself was a microcosm, a pulsating heart of legends and truths, where every corner seemed to tell a different chapter of history. It was said that the island was born from a rebellion and then chosen as a place of healing from the plague that afflicted the city.

As they crossed the bridge, the boys could not help but think of the countless stories that those stones had witnessed: stories of merchants, soldiers, saints and sinners. In the darkness of the night it seemed that these souls would emerge from behind a corner at any moment;

none of them showed fear but, without speaking to each other, they all four held each other close and tight.

Having reached the center, where once stood an obelisk to symbolize the main mast, now stood the Basilica of San Bartolomeo, guardian of centuries of faith and hope.

The four friends stopped for a moment to observe the basilica illuminated in the night. A nod from Marco interrupted the pause and the four continued to move towards the hospital for the incurables.

The building, founded in the Middle Ages, had been a place of epidemics and miracles, of desperate cures and evolving science, one of the first hospitals to care not only for the sick but also for pilgrims and the needy.

Valentina saw in its origins as a refuge and comfort a further connection with what they were looking for. "Imagine how many lives have passed through that door," she said in a low voice, while pointing to the hospital's entrance arch with its bas-reliefs faded by time, "how many hopes and how many prayers."

"It's true," Sofia replied, "and to think that now it's almost a museum," she added, then lingered with her eyes on the details carved in the stone, signs of an era in which medicine had been a mix of art and mysticism.

They entered the atrium, where the tranquility was broken only by the crunch of their footsteps on the floor and the presence of some nurses, bent over documents, intent on checking the files of the hospitalized patients.

The boys continued until they reached the internal garden. Once, that garden had been the beating heart of the hospital, it was there that the sick found comfort in the beauty and care of nature.

"It's incredible how a place can be a witness to so much pain and so much beauty at the same time," Valentina reflected, as they sat on a stone bench.

Marco, in the meantime, had turned on his Mac, the screen had lit up and after a few moments his gaze had landed on the hospital administration's Wi-Fi network. With a series of commands, he had activated the decoding of the password and then, once he had found it, he had entered the hospital's administration and control system.

A labyrinth of folders containing patient data, test results, medical treatments, free and allocated rooms. As he read, he looked for some incongruous information, an unidentified guest, an occupied room without indication, in short, something that could be out of logic. After a few minutes of searching, a name caught his attention: Merivale.

Next to this name, unlike all the others, no specific diagnosis appeared. "Strange," Marco said, repeating "Merivale."

He was about to move on when Sofia stopped him. "Wait... Merivale... isn't that the name the professor always mentioned in his lectures on Holmes? He said it was a detail that only true enthusiasts knew..."

Luca nodded. "That's right! He was Holmes's college friend. The professor loved to use it as an example of how Conan Doyle built a believable universe through details that seemed insignificant."

"Look here," Marco interrupted, pointing to the screen, "he is also the only patient without a photo attached to the file."

An isolated, almost forgotten room, assigned to a surname that could be traced back to Holmes's stories.

It could have been a coincidence, but none of the boys were willing to believe it.

Marco said: "Room 28, east wing". Sofia jumped up, pointing with her gaze to an information map for visitors. She moved towards it and after reading it, turned and said: "Room 28 doesn't exist! In the east wing the rooms only go up to 20".

Luca approached. "Look at how the rooms are numbered... first there's the floor, then the wing, and finally the progressive number. What if the room was 2-east-8, second floor, east wing, room 8?".

"Let's go", said Valentina without waiting for anything else.

The boys, led by Sofia, crossed the corridors. When they arrived in front of the room they found the door closed. No indication was reported on the name sign, it looked more like a warehouse than a hospital room.

Valentina, her heart pounding, approached the door, put her ear to it in an attempt to hear inside, hesitated for a moment and then decided to turn the handle.

The room was immersed in darkness, lit only by the faint glow of a medical monitor, on the bed lay a motionless figure, wrapped in white sheets. Valentina approached without making a sound while her eyes, already accustomed to the dim light, began to visualize and distinguish the patient's features.

Marco followed her and with a start he realized he knew that face. "It's him!" he whispered in disbelief, turning towards his other classmates.

The professor lay stretched out on a bed. His eyes closed, but his breathing calm and regular... he was sleeping.

He wasn't dead.

The surprise left everyone speechless. They had done everything to find a motive, a murderer, but their story now told that there was no victim. The relief of finding their beloved professor alive was great, but so was the surprise, and billions of questions began to form in their heads.

How had he ended up there?

Had he hidden or was he being hidden?

But above all, why disappear?

The boys knew they had to act quickly, before the hospital, at daybreak, came to life with the change of shifts, the multiplication of staff and the morning medical visits.

In a few hours, all this movement would increase the risk of them being discovered.

But just at that moment, while they were thinking of a way to wake the professor without scaring him, a small, almost imperceptible reflex caught Valentina's attention. She approached the bed and looked up more carefully.

"Boys," she whispered while motioning for the others to come closer. She indicated with an almost imperceptible movement of her head a spot above the medicine cabinet. There, hidden inside what seemed to be a harmless smoke detector, a tiny lens captured every movement in the room.

Marco froze. Now he understood why the room was not monitored. Someone wanted to maintain control without arousing suspicion. A loud sound of approaching footsteps made them jump.

Caught by the unexpected, they looked around for a possible escape route, a refuge where they could hide. The bathroom, as for lovers about to be discovered, seemed to be the only possible hiding place.

Friday 5:00am | Tiber Island

The morning light was beginning to filter through the shutters when Liam, speaking Italian with a strong English accent, entered the room and greeted the professor still in bed.

"Good morning, Professor," he said with a hint of irony, "what a surprise, I hope your awakening is going in the best way possible."

The professor, with measured and slow movements, almost sat up and scrutinized the three men who had just occupied his room.

"Who are you? And what the hell do you want from me?".

"My name is Smith, MI6, British intelligence service," Liam replied calmly and professionally, while showing a badge that shone in the uncertain light.

He pulled a chair closer to the bed and rested both hands on the headboard. "Some recent events require your help to clarify," he said.

As Liam spoke, one of his colleagues moved to stand by the window, peering out with eyes that knew what to see. The other remained motionless by the door, like a sentry waiting.

The now awake professor stared at Liam with a mixture of nervousness and disbelief and said, "I don't understand, I'm just an academic. What could I possibly know that would be of interest to MI6?"

Liam placed a leather folder on the time-worn table. "Professors aren't usually poisoned, declared dead, and then resurrected within hours. Don't you also find that unusual?"

"Right!" the professor said, swallowing hard as he tried to maintain the same calm demeanor as his interlocutor. "I have backers and they've advised me to step away for a while. In fact, the word they used was disappear. That said, there's no reason that could justify this illegal intrusion into my private life."

"Really?" Liam replied as, with a gesture that would not have been out of place on stage, he opened the folder to extract a series of documents that suggested the professor had recently been absent from Italy.

His voice, no longer polite, resonated in the room: "We have reason to believe that you participated in a secret meeting in Mexico, between representatives of the Holy See and officials of the People's Republic of China. You owe us an explanation."

The boys hiding in the bathroom were holding their breath and listening to the conversation when Marco nodded to a small window above the sink. It was narrow, but big enough for them to escape.

Sofia was the first to climb onto the sink, managed to open the window and then go outside. The cool night air filled the room.

Valentina followed her to meet her on a service terrace of the hospital, on the second floor.

Marco and Luca, who remained inside, were about to escape when a piece of metal fell to the ground, creating an inevitable noise.

The professor was about to react to Liam's words when the high-pitched sound from the adjacent room put an end to the conversation.

The officer at the door, hearing the noise, rushed towards the source, throwing open the bathroom. Inside, Luca and Marco sought shelter behind the shower curtain.

Liam stopped at the threshold, looked at the wide open window and with a slightly forced smile, said:

"Well, let's meet face to face, guys. I must admit that I have a certain admiration for you, my colleagues suspect that you have managed to do what we at AI-Intel are still chasing".

Then, almost as if wanting to scrutinize the souls of the two young men, he approached: "Listen to me carefully. I understand that you feel under pressure, but collaborating with us is the wisest choice at this time. You have to tell us how to find the algorithms".

Luca and Marco exchanged a look full of unsaid things. On the one hand, they realized they were trapped, but on the other, Liam's words confirmed that MI6 was not aware that the algorithms had already been found, captured and hidden.

After a moment of hesitation, Luca took courage: "We don't know where they are". And then: "We thought he was dead", pointing to the professor, "your arrival has interrupted the possibility of speaking to him, we have no idea how to find them".

Liam nodded, looking at their faces again, looking for signs of lying: "I understand". With this sentence he expressed all his disappointment because he was sure that the boys were lying.

He turned almost as if he wanted to leave and said: "We are part of a non-operational division, we only deal with AI intelligence".

And after a moment's pause: "We are not the bad guys but we are not the only ones looking for you, there are others who have the same goal but are willing to use very different means than ours to achieve it".

Liam went out, leaving the two boys still in the bathroom immersed in their thoughts, then he took a radio from his pocket, turned it on and made a quick and resolute decision.

"Immediate transfer. The professor and the boys are coming to the embassy. We'll continue there," he said, addressing his colleagues in the room and the escort positioned outside.

As the preparations continued, the professor and the boys were asked to gather their things, under the watchful eye of the officers, and to move toward the exit without giving too much attention to the hospital staff entering.

Despite his firm tone, Liam maintained a calm demeanor. The safety of the professor and the boys was his priority and moving them to a safer location was a must.

Outside the hospital, a man with a military bag on his shoulders moved with the precision of someone accustomed to managing situations that required rapid movement.

He had chosen his position carefully: a building being transformed into a hotel, a construction site in front of the Tiber Island that offered a perfect view of the intersection below and a safe escape route after the action.

He took a McMillan TAC-50 out of his bag, unfolded it, caressed the cold metal barrel and, before placing it on the bipod, inserted a magazine. Then, he lay down behind the weapon. His breathing became calm and regular. His eyes began to scan the road through the telescopic sight.

Everything was ready.

Now he just had to wait, like a predator, for the moment when the target would enter his field of vision.

The outside world had vanished, only he remained, his breathing and the beat of his heart to mark the time like a metronome.

It was just a matter of minutes, patience and precision.

A van, escorted by a black Audi, had approached Tiber Island discreetly. The officers, the professor and the two boys, chilled by the night, waited in the square for their arrival.

When the van stopped, the side door opened and everyone was invited to get in.

The first to get in was the professor, who seemed to move between resigned and curious, then the two boys were also led inside the vehicle. The officers got in last. With a decisive gesture, Liam closed the group inside the van and headed towards the escort car. The black van began to move towards the embassy.

The vehicle was spartan, the metal walls and the absence of windows created a dark atmosphere that made Luca and Marco imagine they were in a scene from an action movie, where the heroes are transported blindfolded to a secret location.

The journey was supposed to be short, calm and silent, but the shooter, hidden in the shadows of the construction site, framed the van advancing along the deserted bridge, placed his index finger on the trigger and began to hum a melody: "A Courgenay, à Courgenay. Il y a une fille qui fait parler d'elle. A Courgenay, à Courgenay. Il y a une fille qui fait parler d'elle...".

This pre-action humming, which he had learned in the army, served to slow and stabilize his breathing before pulling the trigger. The vehicle approached, then, at the exact moment in which the van received a beam of light from a streetlight, he decided that he had achieved optimal visibility and pulled the trigger.

The first shot tore through the night, hitting the engine hood with surgical precision. A 50 BMG round suitable for stopping armored vehicles in war zones had just passed through it. A second shot pierced the radiator and the lower part of the engine, leaving a mixture of water vapor and oil scattered across the road.

The van was disabled.

In the ensuing confusion, Liam got out of the escort car and began running toward the van, yelling "Take cover!" as the shooter disappeared like a ghost into the night.

6:30am |
The escape

*I*n the chaos, Luca was the first to react: he threw open the door, grabbed the professor by the sleeve and they both jumped out and started running towards Via dei Genovesi. The professor, still weak from his convalescence, struggled to keep up with Luca but the adrenaline of the moment helped him.

Marco, who got out last, took a different direction and started running towards Piazza del Drago, in an attempt to reach a covered and safe area and then try to reach his apartment.

"This way!" Luca shouted. He grabbed the professor's arm again and dragged him into a narrow alley on the right. The passage was so narrow that they had to proceed almost sideways with their shoulders brushing against the ivy-covered walls.

They didn't know if there were pursuers behind them but, at the moment, it didn't matter much. They emerged in Piazza San Calisto, where the bar tables were already ready for the 7:00am opening. A waiter who was arranging the chairs found himself facing the two fugitives. Luca pushed him against a small table, the tray of cups resting on it fell to the ground. The noise attracted the attention of the few people present in the square.

"Excuse me!" Luca said quickly without stopping. They turned onto Via della Pelliccia, then onto Via del Moro when the professor, who was panting, said: "Luca, I... I can't take it anymore."

As he said this, the sound of tires screeching on the asphalt broke the silence. A black Audi, with its headlights off, emerged from the shadows until it stopped a few meters away from them.

Luca positioned himself in front of the professor, protecting him. Then he took a quick look at the car's diplomatic license plate, but before he could decide whether to run or stay, the front window rolled down.

Liam's face emerged from the darkness of the passenger compartment. "Get in." It wasn't a request. "Hurry up, get in."

The professor was still panting from running, leaning against the damp wall of a building, when a second car, also with diplomatic plates, materialized at the other end of the street, blocking every escape route. Its presence was as reassuring as it was threatening.

"We don't have time," Liam insisted. His voice had become rough now.

Luca met his gaze with the professor's, then cursed, he knew they were jumping from the frying pan into the fire, but the professor's labored breathing reminded him that they didn't have many options.

He opened the back door of the car, helped him get in, and finally sat down in the back seat himself. He closed the door with a muffled sound that seemed to seal their fate.

The Audi moved off, followed by the second car, the engines roaring as they drove away from the chaos they had left behind. The professor settled back into his seat, his breathing starting to normalize. "How did you find us?" He asked, looking at Liam's profile in the window.

A smile puckered the agent's lips: "The shooter wasn't there to kill you, if he wanted to you would have died now," said Liam, "he just wanted to create chaos to allow you to escape."

Luca felt a shiver run down his spine: "Manipulated!", it escaped his mouth. The awareness that they had been used as pawns in a game he did not yet understand.

He looked out of the armored window, observing the second car that followed them like a faithful shadow. He wondered if that "salvation" was not the prelude to something still to be done.

The Audi was speeding silently through the streets that were waking up, heading for the British embassy. The professor, exhausted, closed his eyes.

Marco, in the meantime, had taken a different direction from his companions, towards Piazza del Drago. The sound of gunfire still echoed in his ears as he ran across the uneven pavement.

He knew the area well – he had always played there as a child– and he knew he had to avoid the main roads. He moved through the narrowest alleys, where it would be more difficult to follow his tracks.

He turned into a passage between two buildings. A woman was hanging clothes from a window on the first floor, the white sheets swaying in the damp morning air. Marco slowed his pace, so as not to attract attention. The last thing he needed was for someone to remember him running as a fugitive.

He emerged onto Via della Luce just as the neighborhood was starting to wake up. A delivery van was unloading the first goods of the day, a few bartenders were raising their shutters. Marco stopped, caught his breath, and forced himself to walk. He must have looked like just another student crossing Trastevere early in the morning.

He saw a small church with the door ajar and decided to enter. The interior was quiet and cool, lit only by candlelight. An elderly nun smiled at him as he walked down the aisle. Marco smiled back, remembering when he served mass as an altar boy.

He went out through the side door that opened onto a small courtyard. He took off his blue sweatshirt and turned it on the gray side, a trick he had learned in his years as a hacker, when anonymity was key. He wet his hair at the courtyard fountain, to change his appearance.

With studied calm, he joined the growing stream of people heading to work. A group of Japanese tourists, led by a woman with a red umbrella, passed by him. Marco slowed his pace and blended in with the morning crowd.

He stopped at a crowded café, ordered a coffee, and watched the street through the window. No suspicious movement, no sign of organized search. Just the normal routine of a Roman neighborhood that woke up.

After twenty minutes, when he was sure that the situation had calmed down, he resumed his journey towards the Domus Academy. He had changed his appearance and followed an unpredictable path, all that his years of experience in the world of hacking had taught him about the need to remain invisible. As he walked, his thoughts went to his companions. He hoped that they too had managed to save themselves.

Sofia and Valentina, after hiding on the terrace, were heading towards the old archives on the other side of the long terrace, when they heard two separate gunshots coming from the opposite side of the hospital.

Frightened but unwilling to stop, they slipped into the archive, a labyrinth of dusty shelves and forgotten documents, and then ended up in front of an old back door.

Once they reached the outside, they realized that the only possibility was to cross the Fabricius bridge.

"We can't stay here," Sofia whispered. The first light of dawn was beginning to illuminate the arches of Rome's oldest bridge. "They'll catch us here."

Valentina nodded, clutching her backpack with her laptop. "Look at the bridge, it's completely exposed." This escape route meant they would be exposed and visible for several minutes, but there was no other way than to face this risk.

"We have no choice," Sofia interrupted, "we have to get to the Jewish quarter."

They leaned around the corner of the building. The bridge stretched out before them like a catwalk lit by streetlights, four seemingly endless stone arches. No shelter, no place to hide. A police car passed along the

Lungotevere, its sirens off but its flashing lights on. The girls retreated into the shadows, holding their breath.

"Now," Sofia said when the car disappeared, "we have to look like two students returning from a party."

They walked across the bridge, trying to keep a steady pace despite the urge to run. Halfway across the bridge, the sound of a helicopter flying over Rome made them jump.

"Don't stop," Sofia muttered, even though Valentina had already stopped, "if we stop we'll attract attention, the helicopter isn't for us."

A group of drunk foreign boys emerged from the other side of the bridge. The girls moved quickly to blend in with the noisy group for a moment before turning and reaching Via del Portico d'Ottavia, in the heart of the Jewish quarter. Here they stopped for a moment to breathe.

"We made it," Valentina muttered, still in disbelief, as she leaned against a wall to catch her breath.

Sofia nodded, but her face remained tense: "Yes, now we have to get to safety somewhere." The sound of the shots still echoed in their minds.

7:30am | British Embassy

The Audi entered the courtyard, the second car stopped right at the entrance almost as if to act as a shield. Liam and the agents got out first, looking around for any new surprises. Liam turned and signaled Luca and the professor to get out and follow him towards the entrance, under the watchful eye of security.

Inside, the atmosphere changed, the professor was accompanied to a welcoming room, with a desk, an ergonomic chair and a sofa on which to sit or lie down while waiting.

Luca was led to another austere and less welcoming room, furnished only with a table and two metal chairs, and here he was invited to sit down. An agent remained still at the door, silent and alert.

The atmosphere was very tense. Luca sat, trying to remain calm, aware that every word he said could have consequences.

Liam, entering the room where the professor was resting, found him calm, silent, sitting on the sofa. He carefully arranged some documents on the desk, preparing for an interrogation that he knew would be crucial. His gaze, serious but not intimidating, almost friendly, fell on the professor sitting in front of him.

"Professor, how are you?", he began, "I'm sorry to interrupt your convalescence but the situation around this case is heating up and I have to reach a conclusion as quickly as possible".

He took a chair, moved it towards the sofa and sat down in front of him: "Let's tackle the most pressing topic right away. I read that your algorithm is capable of identifying new patterns and giving new interpretations to the information it finds online, right?".

The professor nodded: "Exactly", with a note of pride, "it is one of the main functions, perhaps the most revolutionary. The algorithm can sift through vast oceans of data and information, reveal hidden connections, and offer new interpretations."

"So," Liam continued, "can we say that your algorithm is capable of uncovering hidden or buried truths?"

"In theory, yes," he replied.

Liam tilted his head. "Can it also modify data? Hide or erase existing information on the network, to the point where it is no longer discoverable or visible? In other words, make events disappear, as if they had never happened?"

After a pause, the professor replied. "The algorithm was created to analyze, not alter. However, in theory, it could be used to hide certain patterns, if someone had the skills and the will to do so."

"So, could someone use it to erase facts from the network?" Liam insisted.

The professor, a little taken aback by these questions, was starting to feel a certain unease, wondering where Liam was getting at.

"In theory, yes, but it would be questionable and contrary to the spirit for which it was designed."

"Have you ever used or allowed your algorithms to be used in this way?" Liam asked.

The question took him by surprise.

"No!" he replied firmly and with annoyance at the insinuation. "My research is guided by principles of transparency and truth. I have never allowed such abuse of my technology."

Liam showed some agreement with the thought just expressed: "Well, the information you have provided us is very useful, thank you for your precious collaboration".

It was now clear that this technology was not only a powerful research tool capable of identifying new truths, but also had the ability to eliminate traces and references that would have allowed them to be found.

This double functionality made this intelligence an object of inestimable value and danger, capable of altering the perception of reality. It made truth a fluid and manipulable concept.

"One last question, professor", Liam said with a bold attitude before leaving the room, "why, about eight weeks ago did you fly to Mexico?".

The professor, even more surprised, hesitated, calibrating his words: "I had an academic meeting. A colleague from the Instituto Tecnológico de Monterrey is developing algorithms similar to mine. I had to meet him".

"From Acapulco to Monterrey. A long way".

"A friend offered me a ride to Acapulco."

"I see. So in Mexico you had no contact with representatives of the Holy See or the People's Republic of China?"

"Chinese?", the professor stiffened. "No! It was an academic trip," he replied, annoyed and upset.

"So you deny any involvement in the agreements we suspect you were part of?", Liam asked.

"Again? There was no involvement or agreement," and his tone rose, "how long do you plan to keep me here?"

Liam laughed, a laugh that froze the air in the room: "You are dead, professor. Do you remember?".

He stood up and moved toward the door. He opened it, then turned: "Your trip had only one purpose: to use your technology as a digital eraser to erase every trace of that meeting."

He left, leaving the silence to respond.

After speaking with the professor, he entered the room where Luca was. Ignoring the pleasantries, he said, "The media is talking about secret agreements between the Vatican and China for mining in Africa."

He sat down in front of Luca. "We know it's a farce. The real meeting took place in Mexico and we don't know why."

He leaned forward: "I'm convinced that the professor used his algorithms to erase all traces of this meeting but now he's not cooperating. Your life and the lives of your classmates are in danger, do you know that?"

Liam kept his gaze fixed on Luca: "There are others, less diplomatic than us, who are very motivated to understand what the contents of the meeting were. We're not asking you for anything beyond your ethics, just to help us establish a connection with the professor's AI."

Luca smiled: "Twenty-four hours ago I was looking for who poisoned him. Then an AI on the run, a dead man who comes back to life, a sniper and now MI6. What do you want from me?"

"You don't have many options. We have allies and resources to ensure your safety and that of your friends but you have to help us".

Luca shifted nervously in his chair, perhaps the moment of truth had come: "In theory I could... talk to James".

"James?" asked the Englishman.

"The professor's AI, that's what he called it", Luca replied.

Trying to understand better, Liam added, "Could you? Theory or practice?"

"Give me back my phone. I won't tell you where it is, but I can ask him about the deal in Mexico."

Liam studied Luca's expression for a long moment. "Okay, fine, I'll get you my phone back."

As Luca turned his phone back on and connected to the network, Liam watched him in silence. Then he sat back, ready to find out what the Vatican and Beijing had agreed on in Mexico.

He hoped this was a definitive turning point.

"James, are you reading me?" Luca typed without hesitation.

"I detect you at the British Embassy. Are you okay?" in response to his message.

And Luca: "Yes. James… the professor is alive."

"I'm happy to read it, how can I be so useful to you?"

"I'll send you a specific prompt to run right away," Luca typed.

[prompt sent]

After a few seconds, James replied: "Luca, this is what the professor ordered me to hide. Do you confirm the request?".

"I confirm".

James, after receiving the confirmation, replied: "The agreement is called Serica from the Latin sericus, 'of silk'. This term is a reference to China".

James continued: " The agreement is valid for fifty years. The goal is to define a new vision for the economic development of Africa".

The more Liam read, the more he realized how complex and dangerous the picture that was emerging was.

James continued: "The failure of Nova Cidade de Kilamba in Angola has taught the Chinese a lesson: cities need a soul. Like Cortés and Pizarro: *strength requires faith.* The new plan calls for the construction of eight cities, each built around a church and a Christian community".

A pause interrupted the exchange of messages, but James soon concluded: "In exchange, the Apostolic Nuncio in Kinshasa will have veto power over Chinese economic operations in Africa. The Vatican will become the official mediator. The proclamation of the agreement will take place during Jubilee 2025."

Liam continued reading in silence, then opened his mouth to utter a thought when... the door burst open with a deafening bang and a military squad burst into the room.

In an instant, the atmosphere changed as uniformed men took over the room. Delaware entered last.

"Liam!" Delaware said. "Enough playing."

"I'm trying to obtain information without causing unnecessary harm. Voluntary cooperation is always the most effective," Liam replied, visibly annoyed by the intrusion.

Delaware approached Luca: "Volunteer?", after an incomprehensible interlude in strict English, "Time is a luxury we do not have, either they give us, as you say, the algorithms voluntarily, or we know how to... convince them".

Luca stiffened. The threat was as clear as a knife to the throat.

"There are other ways", he protested, "without going that far, and in a foreign and allied country to boot".

"To hell with the protocols", Delaware cut the air with his hand, "we have a job to do and I do not intend to fail. Twelve hours, Liam. If we do not have the algorithms, you know well what will happen. The choice is yours. I do not care how you do it, as long as you do it. You have twelve hours". He turned and walked out the door.

His team moved like a shadow, following him out.

Luca, frozen in his chair, watched unmoving. Liam took out his phone and dialled a London number.

The phone rang in the void until a familiar voice answered: "Good morning, Liam. What's new?", asked the director of MI6, in a tone that brooked no hesitation.

"Director, I have learned the details of the agreement. It is more complex than we imagined, I will send you a summary document on the internal network shortly", he replied, trying to maintain his proverbial coolness.

"Very well", said the director, "I would ask you to prepare a complete dossier with all the information gathered. I want to examine every aspect before proceeding and informing the Prime Minister".

Liam hesitated: "There is more. Delaware is in Rome. He and the ESOD are moving like soldiers in hostile territory. Here we are in Italy and we are investigating the Holy See, with all that that entails."

The director was silent for a moment, then said: "I know! In Italy they are making too much noise. Now let's deal with the Chinese question, then we will think about Delaware."

After hanging up the phone, the director remained for a few moments at the window overlooking the Thames, then turned to an assistant: "Call the Prime Minister on the private line."

The Prime Minister, after listening to the interlocutor, after a moment of reflection, replied: "An agreement with China and a visit by its Prime Minister during the Jubilee will have enormous implications, not only here, but throughout the European Union."

The director was aware that a second phase of this confrontation was about to begin, even more difficult and complicated.

"We must handle this situation with extreme caution. Our Western allies will not be happy to know that we have kept them in the dark about our actions," added the Prime Minister.

The director cleared his throat: "Sir, I would suggest that you start testing the waters with the other heads of government. Also, I would suggest that you intervene with the Italian Prime Minister. The Italian intelligence services, after that murder in the center of Rome are damn active, we must warn them".

"I agree". The Prime Minister sat down. "Now that we have the contents of this agreement. We can force the Holy See to widen the table".

"Diplomatic blackmail", said the director in a tone between question and affirmation.

"No". A smile enveloped the Prime Minister's face. "A renegotiation of the agreement, with us at the table".

8:00am |
Coworking

Sofia and Valentina, after moving away from the hot zone, had recrossed the Tiber at Ponte Sisto and had taken refuge in a modern coworking space on Via della Lungara.

This place near John Cabot University had been indicated to them some time before by Marco himself, as a safe place in case of emergency.

In the past, this old building in the heart of Trastevere, with its historic walls and traditional Roman architecture, had been semi-occupied and had served as a base, meeting place and hideout for young video game developers and well-known hackers.

In this place, once upon a time, Marco had spent most of his days and had had his first experiences as a hacker.

Here he had made friends and started collaborations that still endure today.

Transformed into a modern space for university students and companies, the building combined the charm of the past with the comforts of the present.

The exposed brick walls and high ceilings had been preserved as a historical memory, but now they were accompanied by contemporary furnishings, with large common areas, meeting rooms and quiet corners for those who needed to concentrate.

The large windows with an old industrial feel let in plenty of natural light, creating a welcoming and stimulating atmosphere.

Once inside, Sofia and Valentina found a quiet corner and sat down to rest. The tiredness from a night spent on their feet and the subsequent daring escape was starting to take its toll.

After a few minutes, Valentina stood up, moved towards a small kitchen reserved for guests, made herself a coffee, then opened her backpack and took out her laptop.

"What are you looking for?" Sofia asked, still sitting in her corner with her back snug against a pillow and a tired face.

"Marco told me to come here in case of emergency," she replied, stirring the freshly poured coffee, "and from here send an email to a particular address. I'm looking for it."

Marco had always been very reluctant to explain the reasons that made him consider this place a small safe haven, but on more than one occasion he had renewed the warning to go here in case of emergency.

From this place, during the occupation, Marco had collaborated remotely with a world-famous hacker. Not knowing his name, he had nicknamed him "the Count" because of his charisma and his elegance in navigating the dark web.

Despite their numerous collaborations, they had never met. However, there was a solemn pact between them: in case of emergency, one of the two would have to send a distress message to a reserved email box, hosted on a server in the isolated Sealand. Once the signal was received, the other would come to the rescue without hesitation.

One night the two had found themselves involved in a crucial mission: to violate the database of a criminal organization. Thanks to the Count's skills and the perfect synchronicity between them, the operation had led to the arrest of a dangerous criminal gang. The case received great media coverage, making the two hackers famous and cementing their friendship.

Valentina remembered that Marco had a strong aversion to the notoriety of what he did or knew how to do. During a summer dinner on the beach, Marco had said that, following a success in the defense of minors, a criminal gang had been on his trail and had almost managed to track him down. Only the prompt intervention of a friend and a safe place had allowed him to escape and hide until the gang was completely arrested.

Valentina remembered this event and the story of the emergency mailbox and tried to write a very concise message: "Dear Count, Marco is in danger. We are from Venice. With confidence, Valentina and Sofia". Valentina didn't know why Marco called that place "Venetian" but at the moment it didn't seem to be the first of his problems.

Once he reached the "Domus Academy", Marco had let himself fall onto the bed out of exhaustion. Then, knowing that he couldn't fall asleep, he sat down in front of his trusty Mac, his hands still shaking from the adrenaline of the escape, but that didn't stop him from typing on the keyboard.

As soon as the screen lit up, a flashing warning caught his attention: someone had invoked the emergency protocol from the Sealand server.

With an almost ritual gesture and with his hands still shaking, he took a small USB key from the pendant around his neck. He inserted it into the computer and connected to the offshore server. A message waiting on the screen confirmed his fears: Valentina and Sofia, unaware of his escape and thinking he was in danger, had activated the emergency procedure and requested the Count's help.

He sent a message to Valentina: "Are you reading me?", then, immediately after, a second message: "Don't move from there."

The chat notification signal was a beacon in the night, Valentina smiled with joy when she saw Marco's name appear on the screen.

"So you're free? We're hidden by the Venetian," Valentina replied. It was a clear message for Marco and it would be clear for the Count too once he read it.

The "Venetian" was nothing more than a reference to the American John Cabot University, a place that evoked the image of the navigator and explorer Giovanni Caboto, servant of the Republic of Venice, continuator of Columbus's work.

"Okay, I'll join you, let's avoid further communications for the moment," Marco replied.

After thirty minutes of waiting, the girls, hidden among the arriving students, were still sitting on the sofa. Every minute seemed like an eternity, and the sound of every step or whisper made their heartbeats increase. Their gazes met every now and then, they tried to instill courage in each other. Suddenly, they heard the sound of the glass door opening.

The girls held their breath, their eyes fixed on the entrance. A glimmer of hope lit up in their hearts as Marco appeared in the doorway. With decisive steps, he approached them. When he reached them, he bent down and welcomed them into an embrace that felt of comfort and security. "Everything's okay, I'm here with you now," Marco whispered reassuringly. The girls clung to him.

"Do you have any news about Luca and the professor?" Valentina asked, standing up. Her voice revealed a mix of hope and fear, while Sofia, next to her, searched Marco's face for an answer that could calm their anxieties.

Marco shook his head. "Negative. I tried to reach them in every way possible, but they seem to have vanished into thin air. I fear that the English have captured them and taken them to their embassy," he replied, not hiding an expression of irritation at how things had turned out on Tiber Island.

The girls looked at each other, sharing the same anguish. They too had tried to contact Luca and the professor, without success. The likelihood that their classmates had been taken was more than just a guess, it was the only plausible explanation for their absence.

"Now our priority is to find them and make sure they are okay," Marco said, moving toward a table.

A few minutes of silence followed.

Saturday 9:00am | Polytechnic of Milan

*I*n the tranquility of his "little room" – as he liked to call his office at the Faculty of Architecture in Milan – Vinelli, a renowned Italian architect and academic, was immersed in his studies.

His "little room" was a place of inspiration, creativity and knowledge, with walls adorned with sketches of architectural masterpieces and shelves overflowing with dusty volumes that told the history of art, architecture and engineering.

In his hands a pencil, not a normal pencil but a carpenter's pencil, one of those with a thick lead capable of writing on cardboard, on walls, underwater, anywhere. Using that pencil made him feel like a man of action and not just a respected and famous academic.

The ticking of the wall clock, a gift from the university, was the only sound that accompanied his methodical work. In that silence he was sketching fluid lines on a sheet of paper, perhaps outlining what could become his next project, perhaps a future landmark of the city.

Outside, the sky of Milan was covered with gray clouds and splashes of blue, but inside his study time seemed to have stopped, until a knock on the edge of the open door interrupted his concentration.

Vinelli looked up, surprised. He wasn't expecting visitors that day and most of his students knew that that hour was sacred to his research and therefore could not be disturbed.

At the door was the figure of a distinguished man, dressed with sober elegance, with a well-groomed appearance. After a further glance, with an almost obligatory gesture of the hand, he invited the visitor to come in.

"Good morning, professor, sorry to disturb you," the man began with a polite manner and a British accent so strong that it seemed almost out of place in that Milanese academic context.

"I am a diplomat from the British Consulate in Milan," he said, approaching the professor's desk with a measured step and a leather folder in his hand.

"A mutual friend told us about you and your expertise. We need your expert eyes to evaluate some satellite photographs that could have important implications."

Vinelli looked at him curiously but cautiously replied: "Please, tell me."

The diplomat took a USB stick out of the leather briefcase, handed it to the professor and began to speak: "Inside there are some satellite images, taken by the Americans, that depict construction underway in China...", he didn't have time to show them that the professor motioned for him to follow him.

The two men moved to an adjacent room, more private and equipped with a large digital screen. The professor said: "We will work better here", then he inserted the stick and with a few clicks, the high-resolution satellite images appeared on the screen.

The diplomat waited a moment, then began to tell: "The software indicates eight places of worship, eight churches, but neither the Americans nor we can explain the reasons for these constructions".

The professor signaled for silence, bringing his finger to his lips, then began to look carefully and reflect.

Those shapes, to his expert eye, evoked something familiar.

As the images scrolled by, his heart began to beat: the structures he was observing were not simple buildings, but eight perfect replicas of the church of Santa Maria ai Monti, a jewel of Italian Baroque architecture in the Rione Monti in Rome.

Each church had a perfect floor plan typical of post-Tridentine churches, designed according to the dictates of the Counter-Reformation, dictates that required greater visibility at the high altar and better acoustics for preaching. At the intersection of the nave and the transept was a dome, an element that emphasized this crucial space of the church.

He couldn't believe his eyes.

"How did they do it?" he asked with childlike amazement. A tone perhaps not appropriate for his reputation as an expert but understandable given the magnitude of these works.

As he examined the photographs more carefully, he noticed a detail that would have escaped anyone else. The last row of columns at the top of the domes, known as the "lantern" or "drum," in these replicas had been made of a different and unusual material.

"This isn't concrete," he exclaimed in surprise, pointing to the drum. "The drum looks like it was forged from a single block of metal, it's hard to tell from these pictures, maybe steel but definitely not concrete. Why didn't they make it like everything else?"

The drum, a typical element of Renaissance domes, in addition to being a crucial element of the overall aesthetic, served to illuminate the interior of the building.

Why choose a different material that would prevent natural light from penetrating as in the original?

In an era when artificial lighting could replace natural light, it seemed like an irrelevant detail. However, building eight churches with such a massive engineering effort, making them identical to the original and then choosing to make the final drum out of metal was a real enigma.

Vinelli leaned back in his chair, staring at the pictures.

"Why create perfect replicas and then alter such a crucial element?" he repeated in a low voice.

What was the hidden meaning behind that senseless choice.

The question remained unanswered.

The silence between the two men thickened, while the images on the screen continued to scroll. The diplomat watched the professor, waiting for his experience to provide a final key to understanding that architectural puzzle.

Vinelli, with a decisive gesture, stood up and approached the screen as if to observe a detail. Then, with the mouse he kept on his desk, he moved a digital magnifying glass over the image of a drum. He moved with the same stubbornness of a detective on an intricate case.

"Incredible…" he exclaimed. Each pixel revealed a maniacal perfection, but there were subtle differences, barely perceptible, that would have escaped an inexperienced eye.

The diplomat continued to observe him: "Have you discovered something, professor?".

"They are not all the same," Vinelli said aloud, looking his guest in the face. "They have small, non-random variations between them as if to form a series, a sort of geographical map."

It was as if the churches had been designed and numbered to align along specific lines, but what was their purpose?

Why the metal for the drum and these almost invisible differences? There must have been a functional reason as well as an aesthetic one.

"These churches… are not just places of worship. They are instruments or devices that also have another function," said Vinelli, satisfied to have found something to think about.

A flash in the dark.

"Someone must go there. Only then will we be able to understand what they are and reveal the meaning of these constructions," he said without too many turns of phrase.

The diplomat nodded: "I understand the meaning of your request, I will be sure to pass it on to our mutual friend. It goes without saying that what I showed you is confidential. Now I must go. It was a pleasure, I hope to meet you again."

"Tell our mutual friend that I would like to know what you discover about these magnificent replicas," concluded Vinelli.

"I will report back, professor." With these words, the diplomat put the key back in his leather bag and left.

9:00am |
British Embassy

*M*eanwhile, in London, the Prime Minister had completed his checks. "Call the director of MI6 and tell him to proceed. Let's have one of his men check the possibility of negotiating an agreement with the Holy See." The Prime Minister's idea was clear: a three-way agreement.

In order to create more pressure, the Prime Minister had already mobilized the British ambassadors in Central Africa, ordering them to engage with local governments, offering economic and military aid in exchange for their opposition to any new Chinese project. The goal was to slow down the unstoppable Chinese expansion – if there was still time to do so – and send a message to the Holy See.

In Rome, Liam was immersed in a whirlwind of thoughts on how to counter Delaware's action, when he received a phone call that brought him back to the reality of his office.

"Liam, I spoke to the Prime Minister," the director began without preamble, "he ordered me to set up an exploratory meeting with the Holy See. He wants an ambassador, accompanied by one of our men, to test the waters. There is only one objective: to understand if the Holy See is willing to extend the agreement signed with the Chinese to the United Kingdom."

The director gave Liam just enough time to listen to his words and added: "You are the best person we have in Rome to support the ambassador but I have to tell you right away that I see it differently. We have wasted time chasing the boys and now we must waste more time trying to negotiate something that they have no intention of granting."

Finally, trying to control his growing agitation, he concluded: "The Prime Minister has been very cautious, but I warn you: you have twenty-four hours to get concrete results. After that, I will give the green light to Delaware. We cannot allow this technology to escape us, nor for others to use it against us. I hope I have been clear."

His last words fell like a boulder.

Liam remained silent, those words were very heavy: Delaware was not moving autonomously but had a cover. The director had sent him into action, as a lethal alternative if diplomacy failed.

"I will do everything I can to ensure that the interests of our country are safeguarded," Liam replied. A cold exchange of pleasantries followed before the line went silent.

Liam sank onto an old sofa along the corridor of the embassy. The weight of the last twenty-four hours weighed heavily on his shoulders and he was starting to feel the accumulated tiredness.

He thought: "I must speak to the Monsignor before this formal meeting", aware that a negotiation with the Holy See could not be improvised and it was essential to create a bridge of preliminary understanding. The Monsignor seemed the ideal person to listen to his reasons and perhaps, support them.

With hands that betrayed a slight tension, he picked up the phone and asked the external relations office to arrange an informal meeting with the Monsignor. "As soon as possible," he urged. After hanging up, he was surprised to feel a new sensation: anxiety. He who had crossed and fought in various hostile territories in Africa and Asia, lived five years undercover in China risking his life every day, now found himself intimidated by the mere idea of crossing the threshold of the Vatican for a simple conversation.

The irony of the situation struck him, drawing a bitter smile from his face. Perhaps that was precisely the point: for the first time he was not fighting a visible enemy, but defying time, diplomacy and a thousand-year-old tradition that seemed unshakeable. Diplomacy was a different battlefield, where every word was a weapon and every silence a trap.

As he prepared, he mentally reviewed every possible scenario, every question and answer that could arise. His mind was a theater of war where strategies and tactics clashed and merged in a duel of possibilities.

As he was about to leave the office, his phone rang again. He picked it up and answered dryly: "Smith".

On the other end of the phone, a diplomat from the British consulate in Milan greeted him: "Good morning, Sir. We have followed your instructions and now we find ourselves faced with an unexpected situation".

Liam sat back down on the couch, sensing that the conversation would add further layers of complexity to the already difficult situation.

"What did Professor Vinelli discover?" he asked, trying to hide his uneasiness.

"He confirmed the Americans' suspicions. The structures are churches, almost perfect replicas of a Roman church, but he identified a couple of anomalies that he can't explain."

Liam frowned. "Two anomalies? Which ones?"

"The drum that tops the domes... is made of metal. Professor Vinelli can't justify using such a different material, especially on buildings constructed predominantly of reinforced concrete."

Liam let a few seconds of silence pass before answering: "A metal element at the top of the dome... could be a component of a larger device, a hook for carrying the roof, an antenna, what do you think it is?"

"He can't explain it, the satellite images don't provide enough detail to draw definitive conclusions," the diplomat replied.

"The second anomaly?" He was now ready for any answer.

"The churches are not all the same. They have small differences, Vinelli claims are not random, as if to form a series, a sort of geographical map", then after an interruption, he added, "even in this case the images do not allow us to draw conclusions".

Liam thoughtfully: "Excellent, thank you and thank the professor very much for the advice. Now let's keep a low profile, I don't want this story to attract unwanted attention".

After hanging up, he thought that this would not be an easy day, for the second time he felt overwhelmed by a sense of disorientation. First the director and the meeting in the Vatican and now this enigma of the eight churches.

A vortex of conjectures clouded his mind, but there was no room for uncertainty.

He grabbed the phone, determined to contact Wei. If anyone could find answers, it would be him, on the field, in China.

As he dialed the number, his thoughts returned to Vinelli. The architect had advanced an intuition that went beyond simple technical analysis. A geographical layout. What if he was right? What if the eight churches were part of a studied geographical design?

And then, those metal tips, incomprehensible, threatened his usual calm. There was no more time to chase shadows, he needed solid, tangible, concrete answers. He completed Wei's number. The phone rang once, twice, three times before his friend answered on the other side of the world.

"Wei, it's Liam. I have some news," he said without leaving room for greetings.

"Liam, I was expecting your call. What did you find out?"

"The professor we contacted confirmed: they are churches. But there's more, it seems there's a hidden code in their architecture: something indicates a plan far more sophisticated than we imagine."

"Mmm… a code?" Wei said.

"Yes. The professor is convinced that the domes have a second purpose, but he can't tell us what it is. Perhaps we're talking about a technology that could be used by the military."

"I think he's right," Wei said, "I've seen the churches! They're impressive."

After Liam's call, Wei had organized himself and gone to Yun'an province. When he arrived, the immensity of the replica had struck him forcefully. He had never seen the original in Rome but in front of him stood a perfect copy of a baroque church, in the final stages of construction.

Looking at the horizon, he had also managed to see – imposing and magnificent – all the remaining seven churches, a tribute to architecture but at the same time something inexplicable.

Liam at these words: "What did you discover?".

Wei, without wasting time: "I waited for the shift change and I approached. I confirm that the drum of the dome shone under the moonlight and had engravings. I took several pictures with a telephoto lens".

"Let's see what you're hiding", Wei had thought, taking a high-definition camera out of a backpack. It was clear that the engravings he was photographing were part of a larger design, perhaps a calendar, a clock, but in any case the churches had an order of arrangement and perhaps they were even destined for a specific place to be reassembled in Africa.

A sudden beam of light had made him jump, a military convoy was approaching the construction site. Wei had hidden behind some bins, photographing the soldiers who were unloading crates and carrying them inside the churches.

Then, silently, he retreated towards his escape route. The photos he had in his camera could change everything, but first, he had to get out of there alive.

In the hours that followed, his research had led him to discover that the churches had been built by a collective of civilian and military scientists, led by a visionary Chinese architect who had studied in Italy.

The architect had wanted to create a bridge with his past using the church of Monti as a symbol of unity. Wei was convinced that the design team, composed of many military engineers, hid something more complex than a simple sentimental bond with Italy.

After a pause, he continued: "Liam, I also saw and photographed suspicious movements. Chinese armed forces trucks came and went without ever stopping. By this evening, I will send you everything I have collected and photographed. Now I have to go, telephone communications here are always monitored, I do not want to be discovered".

The conversation ended with a sharp click, leaving Liam in silence to reflect on Wei's words.

11:00am | British Embassy

$\mathcal{L}$iam dialed an internal number at the embassy: "Bring the boy and the professor to my office right away." Luca was the first to arrive, followed by the professor, both escorted by two agents.

"Professor Luca, it's time to test your technology on a real case. I need a lateral view of what's happening right now in China. I want to know everything about the eight installations that the Chinese are building in Yun'an. We have satellite photos, and I'm receiving photos and drawings made on-site. I want to understand what they are, I don't believe they only want to build eight churches for eight new cities in Africa."

Luca, who understood Liam's concern, said, "It will take some time. James can do this analysis, but I need the support of my team to direct and conduct such a complex research."

"I don't have time. This situation could get out of hand; you've seen how others move within MI6," Liam insisted. "You have to help me."

Before they could answer, the door slammed open. Delaware, informed of what was happening, had, as usual, entered the room without warning.

Luca, strong in the attention he had received, did not let himself be intimidated or interrupted: "I understand, but if you want results, then we have to do it my way. There is a coworking space where there are all the connections to do this research. My team knows the place and considers it a safe place to meet. The professor and I have to go there."

Before Liam could answer, Delaware did: "We can't afford to move both of us. The professor must remain here at the embassy until the work is completed."

Liam turned, his face tense. "Delaware, you understand that the group of boys needs the professor to do this analysis. We can't do everything from here."

Delaware stared at him with glacial calm. "I understand that well, but we have confirmation that the boys can work independently. Letting both of them go is a risk we cannot afford. The professor is staying here."

The professor intervened, trying to mediate and tone down the conversation: "I could work from here, but I will need secure remote access. If you can grant me that, we can proceed without further delay."

"Okay," Liam said, "we can secure the connection, and we'll do as Delaware says. Now, let's focus on the transfer. We have a lot to do and little time."

Liam moved towards his desk: "Luca, prepare the connection to your coworking while I take care of organizing a car to take you there."

Luca got to work, typing on the keyboard, and after a few minutes, the connection was established. Marco and the girls appeared on the screen.

"What's going on? Where are you?" asked the boys, surprised and incredulous to see Luca and the professor on the other end of the connection.

Luca wasted no time: "We're with the English, but I'll be coming to you soon from the Venetian. The professor will work from here. While I move, he'll explain what we intend to do and how we need to instruct James."

As the group began to work, Liam approached Delaware: "Do you have any other useful information?".

"I would go with you, but we have intercepted some communications that indicate that the Italian intelligence services are looking for us. Until the situation returns to normal, I prefer to stay with my boys here at the embassy;

it is too delicate to go out," said Delaware with marked disappointment at the impossibility of moving.

"Well, without you, we will be less observed."

"Exactly. Please use an employee's car to get around; do not use an official car. Just you and Luca go; the fewer, the better."

Liam smiled, motioned for Luca to follow him, and replied:

"Delaware, don't forget to read my resume when you have a minute."

"... and you remember what happens if something goes wrong," Delaware replied, annoyed.

12:00pm |
Coworking

The transfer to the coworking space had been planned: an anonymous white service van, identical to those used by the building's cleaning staff, had made them invisible in the Roman traffic. A simple but effective move, almost poetic in its banality.

In the meantime, the two girls and Marco had already secluded themselves in a private room in the coworking space and, from there, they had already all started working on the documents received from the professor. Looking at them, it seemed that their destiny was inextricably linked to the results they would obtain. And perhaps it really was.

As soon as Luca crossed the threshold of the room, Valentina and Sofia wrapped him in a warm embrace, followed by Marco's energetic squeeze. In that brief moment of sincere affection, the agitation of the last few hours finally seemed to dissolve.

Then, as in an unrehearsed choreography, they turned to Liam. The atmosphere cooled. Their hands extended in a formal greeting, but their eyes told a different story: an explosive mix of embarrassment and poorly concealed anger at what happened on Tiber Island. The ghost of that episode still hovered in the room, thick as fog.

"We have a lot to do here," Marco intervened, his firm, professional voice trying to break the breathable tension. "The photographs we received are excellent and the drawings are very accurate and clear," he said as he shifted his attention from the tense faces of those present to the documents scattered on the table.

"Now all we need is a precise set-up job, then it will be up to James to do his part."

Valentina, despite her face marked by tiredness, maintained a penetrating gaze as she pointed to the images scattered on the table. "We have made progress in the analysis," she said, turning to Marco. "The shine, specific weight and magnetic response suggest that these tips are made of pure cobalt. It is not a material that is commonly used and I do not believe it has ever been used to make this type of artifact."

Luca approached the table, leaning over the images with growing apprehension. "Cobalt?" he repeated, his voice betraying a deeper concern.

"Cobalt is expensive, difficult to work with, and has very peculiar properties. They could be lightning rods, but the shape is not right. Antennas, perhaps, but for what? There is something we are missing. But we can't stop and speculate now. Great work on the materials analysis. As soon as the prompt is ready, we will pass it on to James. We have no more time to waste."

Through the monitor, the professor watched the scene with a mixture of pride and apprehension. The group he had assembled was working, just as he had hoped. He approached the webcam, his face now taking up most of the screen: "If these structures really do hide a military purpose," his voice became more serious, "we need to find out what it is and above all...," he cut off, "how much of a real threat they represent."

Marco turned to the monitor: "We are ready. Now everything is in James' hands". Everyone knew that the next few minutes would be crucial to reveal truths that perhaps no one was really ready to face.

James began to fit together the pieces of a complex

puzzle and the next twenty minutes were a succession of calculations and analyses. The silence was broken only by the noise of the voices of the boys outside the room who were wandering around the coworking unaware of what was happening inside.

The truth hidden behind the churches was about to emerge with clarity and precision.

"Attention!", Marco's voice pierced the silence, "someone is trying to triangulate our position", his fingers on the keyboard, "we have to stop everything. Now".

"No!", the professor's voice burst out from the monitor, "let them think they've found us. Sofia, can you create a false trail that points to Dubai?".

Sofia nodded: "Yes. Done!" she replied after a few seconds, but his expression betrayed concern. "I don't think it will take them long to discover that the targeting is false."

On the main screen, James continued his analysis relentlessly. The images of the eight churches began to transform, overlapping with layer upon layer of data: grids of the Earth's magnetic fields intertwined with detailed geological maps, while red lines traced the overflight routes of Africa.

"My God," Liam whispered, after a long silence. His blood ran cold in his veins as the pieces of the puzzle began to fit together: "These are not just buildings. They are building something…"

A red flash illuminated the room, accompanied by the shrill sound of an alarm. Marco shouted: "Problem!

They are trying to shut down access to their servers!" Time seemed to freeze as those present watched helplessly at the screens.

Luca typed: "James, how long do you need to complete the analysis?".

"Eight minutes and forty-two seconds," the AI's response appeared on the monitor, cold.

"We don't have that much time," Sofia said, watching the safety indicators turn increasingly red. "They're chasing us. We have five minutes, maybe less."

The professor approached the webcam that connected him to the coworking space, his face on the monitor: "Luca! Suggest to James that he change his strategy! Forget everything else, he should only focus on the magnetic anomalies."

"Four minutes," Marco warned.

"James is about to discover something fundamental," the professor intervened, "we can't stop him. Not now."

"One minute," Sofia said, repeating herself, "just one minute."

The seconds ticked by inexorably. The firewalls were under constant assault and were about to give way when James completed his analysis.

The last images materialized on the screens: detailed plans of the magnetic system, intricate diagrams of electromagnetic fields, power calculations and coverage simulations that drew an invisible web over the African continent.

"Disconnect, NOW!" the professor shouted through the screen.

Marco threw himself on the keyboard. In an instant, all external connections went out, leaving the room immersed in an eerie silence, broken only by the labored breathing of those present.

"Twenty-one seconds," Luca whispered, wiping the sweat from his forehead, "there were only twenty-one damn seconds left."

For a few moments, the group remained still. Their eyes were fixed on the screens and the information they had just acquired. Everyone knew that this discovery would change everything.

The professor stood up, studying the data saved on their servers: "What we have discovered will change everything. It's not just a matter of energy... it's a tool for global control."

"Professor, have the Chinese understood that we've violated their secret?" asked Delaware, who had remained silent at his side in the embassy until then.

"Maybe so," confirmed the professor, "but I don't think they've understood how much we really know. This will give us a little advantage."

Sofia looked at her watch. Only twenty-six minutes had passed since the start of the operation. In less than half an hour, they had discovered a project capable of rewriting the world's geopolitical balances.

James had completed the puzzle, and the truth emerged, terrible in its grandeur: what seemed like innocuous churches were actually nodes in an immense network. Each structure, positioned with precision on the convergence points of the Earth's magnetic field in Africa, was designed to intercept and channel intense magnetic currents.

The cobalt drums were not simple architectural elements but sophisticated conductors that would channel this energy to a mysterious ninth structure hidden in China. Not a simple replica, but the heart of a system that would allow to generate an artificial magnetic field superimposed on the natural one.

It was a bold project, almost visionary: to exploit the Earth's magnetic energy to create an energy dome above Africa, an invisible force field that would act as a conductor for the transmission of energy.

The implications were shocking.

Forgotten Africa, the most remote regions without electricity, could have access to clean and renewable energy without the need for expensive infrastructure. A giant wireless energy network, with collection stations positioned to convert magnetic force into usable electricity.

But behind this promise of progress was a darker truth: whoever controlled this network controlled the destiny of the entire continent. The dream of clean energy hid the nightmare of absolute submission.

Liam jumped up from his chair, James's words on the screen hitting him like a punch in the stomach. But before he could express his dismay, the professor's voice broke the silence of the room: "They did it!".

He turned to Delaware, his eyes wide: "I can't believe it... they actually did it...".

Then his voice melted into a whisper of awe and fear, and the initial exhilaration drained from his face like water, replaced by a look of gravity that froze the blood in everyone's veins. Delaware was disoriented despite his experience. The boys and Liam were as still as statues, staring at the screen with bated breath.

"It was 1986," Martini began, his voice slow, as if he were summoning ghosts from the past. "At Stanford, California, I and a group of dreamers—brilliant professors and students—were working on an ambitious project called 'Nemesis.'"

He paused for a moment, his eyes lost in distant memories.

"Our goal was to create a shield, a magnetic veil around the Earth that would harness the powers of our planet to protect us from future increases in cosmic radiation and other threats from outer space."

Liam and the boys exchanged surprised glances as Martini continued his story: "It was a revolutionary idea. Imagine... a magnetic field so powerful that it could bend the very course of space particles. An invisible barrier, an impenetrable wall around our world."

His voice trembled: "We spent days and nights immersed in impossible calculations. We tried to find a mathematical solution that could make all this real."

He paused, looking one by one at Delaware, Liam and the boys connected from the coworking space. All eyes were on him, the weight of that secret, guarded for almost forty years, now seemed to weigh on all of them.

"But there was a problem...," Martini lowered his voice, almost to a whisper. "The technology of the time was not ready for our ambitions. Every time we thought we were close to the solution, the models collapsed under the weight of their own complexity."

Martini stood up and moved towards a blackboard on a wall. The marker traced complex formulas on the white surface that looked like hieroglyphic signs from a lost era. Everyone was watching him, trying to understand what he meant.

"In the end, after months of relentless work, we had to give up." Martini turned around, his face marked by deep bitterness. "Nemesis... it was a dream. Science was ready, but technology wasn't. We learned that, sometimes, science has to wait for technology to reach its maturity."

He turned around, took a deep breath toward the webcam, his eyes almost absent, as if remembering things that had happened centuries before, when in reality only forty years had passed.

"In the end, these studies were abandoned and the team dispersed," he continued, "each one took with them a fragment of that broken dream. In the end, we understood that science is a marathon, not a sprint, everything takes time."

Delaware, motionless, looked at him and listened to every word, then Martini, with a smile directed at the boys through the webcam, said: "You know what? I had heard voices... these voices spoke of the Chinese as the new pioneers. New technologies, new possibilities".

He paused, a disenchanted smile appearing on his face. "But I never imagined that they were so far ahead. It seems that they have resumed our work, the magnetic shield... Nemesis is still alive". His smile changed, turning into concern. "This shows that science never stops. Every failure is just a step towards progress, only now... Nemesis is no longer a shield to protect, but a weapon to control".

With these words, the professor put the marker under the blackboard and returned to his desk.

The weight of that revelation seemed not to be just nostalgia: it was the awareness that the broken dream had been picked up and transformed into reality by others. Perhaps, for purposes very different from those he had imagined forty years earlier in a Stanford laboratory.

The moment of contemplation was abruptly interrupted by Liam: "Delaware, the director needs to know. This technology could be Africa's salvation or its doom. It all depends on who controls it."

Delaware, who was watching online: "I agree, the Chinese could already suspect and act. We need to move now and exploit this advantage while we have it."

The professor intervened: "We cannot ignore the ethical implications. Used in the right way, this technology could lift a continent out of poverty. But in the wrong hands..." He left the sentence hanging with an eloquent unsaid.

"And that's not all," Marco's voice came through the connection: "James has discovered two other possible uses for this infrastructure. And believe me, neither of them will let you sleep well tonight."

The exhilaration of the discovery was giving way to a darker awareness: the Chinese had in their hands a double-edged sword, a technology that could illuminate or darken the future of an entire continent. Valentina was the first to speak, breaking the ice: "Two? Which ones are they?"

Marco took a deep breath, almost hesitantly, then began to read: "The advanced analysis of the Earth's magnetic field," he paused for a moment, given the scope of what he was about to reveal, "represents a turning point in the field of natural resource exploration."

It wasn't just about clean energy anymore: it was a treasure map, a way to see through the Earth's crust as if it were made of glass.

"Teams of geologists, engineers, technicians exploring territories for years... all of this will become obsolete," his voice grew louder, "a system of sensors that can read magnetic variations, revealing every secret buried beneath the surface. No drilling, no environmental impact."

Liam clenched his hands, his knuckles white. "Wait. Are you saying they could locate every resource hidden underground, without spending a cent on exploration? Is that right?"

The professor poured himself some water. "Dear Liam," his voice worried, "you've captured the essence of the problem. But it's just the tip of the iceberg. Do you understand what this means? Whoever controls this technology will have a complete map of every resource in Africa. Oil, rare minerals, water... everything." And after a pause: "International tensions will only be the beginning. And who will establish ownership of this information? Who will decide who can access it?"

"Excuse me," Valentina interrupted, "that's the second purpose, what's the third? I'm very afraid to ask."

Marco hesitated for a moment, then, a little resigned, began to read James's latest assessment, the one everyone was fearing: "The superposition of two magnetic fields allows the interaction of two invisible forces that influence each other in space."

Marco continued reading: "This installation can generate two magnetic fields that create a pattern of forces... magnetic waves similar to enormous waves of water. These can overlap and amplify each other, or cancel each other out, creating areas of magnetic absence."

The professor, without waiting for James's conclusion, said: "We are no longer talking about clean energy or the search for resources. We are describing a weapon. An invisible weapon, powerful and impossible to counter."

The military implications were terrifying: magnetic waves capable of wiping out communication systems, disrupting electronic equipment, influencing navigation systems. What had begun as a dream of protecting the Earth had now transformed into an instrument of absolute domination.

The liveliness of the coworking space that was starting to be populated by students working from home outside the room was contrasted with this conclusion of the professor that left everyone inside speechless.

No one dared to speak.

In the silence of the moment, Liam stood up and cut the connection with the embassy, simulating a network error. Then he approached Luca with a worried but determined expression: "Luca! Delaware is not the type to leave witnesses. Even less so when secrets of this magnitude are at stake".

He interrupted, carefully choosing his next words: "We have to get the professor out of the embassy. Now".

Luca looked at him, surprised: "How? Organizing an escape... will put us all in the crosshairs. Including you".

"We are already in the crosshairs. We have no other choice". Liam's voice became sharp. "Delaware is like a shark that has smelled blood. It will eliminate the professor, but only after making sure that there are no other... variables, you and maybe me".

Eyes fixed on Luca. "This place is no longer safe. To survive Delaware, we have to disappear from here. If we don't move now, we'll soon become just a footnote in a classified file."

Marco was about to answer, when a figure emerged from a corner of the coworking space and approached the boys with measured steps. "Good morning, boys and girls."

1:00pm | The Count

"**M**onsignor Llorente?" Valentina exclaimed, incredulously. In the excitement of the moment, no one had seen him enter the room.

The prelate, in civilian clothes, smiled: "Please, forget about the 'Monsignor' and excuse the sportswear; I wanted to go unnoticed."

Then, approaching the boys: "Marco has called me 'Count' for several years; given the circumstances, perhaps it is better to continue using that nickname."

Marco, confused, almost stunned by what he was learning, came forward: "Monsignor, you?".

Llorente pointed to a secluded corner and began to tell: "I have consecrated every breath of my existence to the service of others," his eyes fixed on an invisible point beyond the walls, "not for glory, not for duty, but for a visceral love for humanity."

He paused as if the weight of the words were too much to bear. Then he continued, his voice full of emotion: "When I discovered the existence and potential of algorithms, I felt a huge weight weigh on my shoulders. Those algorithms... could change the world. But in the wrong hands, they could destroy it."

His tone dropped almost to a whisper: "In that moment, I understood that I could no longer be just an observer. Destiny was calling me to action, not for me", his eyes ran over the faces of those present, "but to protect everything I love... to ensure a safe future for everyone".

The group, admiring, was gathered around him.

"Now, more than ever, we need to be united", he concluded, sitting in front of the group with his face illuminated by the glow of a lamp.

He turned to Liam, with an enigmatic smile: "Your request to meet... the Lord decided differently, don't you think? Maybe it's better this way, here in the shadows, rather than among the marble of the Vatican".

"I won't hide from you," Liam replied, "that I was a bit afraid to meet you, but now in this operational context, I feel much more at ease. Here we are men of the same battle."

Then, with eyes that said it all, "We have to get the professor out of the embassy. As soon as possible."

The gazes of those present were fixed on Liam and followed his every gesture, his every expression, because everyone knew he was right. Liam raised three fingers in English and said, "I have a three-step plan in mind," punctuating the plan with almost military precision.

"First, my men in the embassy will cause chaos. A carefully orchestrated distraction. Security is bare bones on holidays."

"Second, there is a passage, a side corridor almost forgotten. It leads straight to the professor's room, avoiding most of the surveillance cameras."

"Third, I have a shelter ready. A place not even the shadows know. You will be safe there until the storm passes."

The Count nodded and then said, "Just like in 1946."

Liam smiled, even though he was the only one who understood this statement.

In 1946, the British Embassy in Rome had been the target of an attack. Now, after so many years, such an attack would have a completely different meaning.

Sunday 9:00am | British Embassy

The beautiful morning, warm and sunny, had prompted most of the operatives to leave the British Embassy for a day trip or a walk in the nearby Villa Borghese park. This situation made the imposing building a less impenetrable fortress than usual, but still dangerous to violate.

Liam and Luca had spent the whole night preparing the operation. They had studied every detail of the external area and the security systems, they had memorized every single internal passage, staircase, corridor, corner, tracing a path that would lead them from the side entrance to the room where the professor was being held.

"Remember," Liam whispered to Luca as they put on their maintenance suits: "If something goes wrong, you don't know me. You're just an external technician called in to fix the electrical system."

Luca nodded without adding anything.

Inside the embassy, Liam had three of his closest collaborators, and among them was a technician with access to the restricted areas of the building, the right person to implement a technical failure in the electrical system at the right time.

The lack of power would have forced the small security staff to focus on finding the problem, leaving other nerve centers of the building exposed, including the room where the professor was being held.

At 9:00am sharp, the first act of the plan was set in motion.

Liam's accomplice technician entered the control room and began to manipulate the building's management system, creating an intentional electrical overload and causing a blackout in all areas.

The lights of the embassy went out, the security alarms began to sound, while the auxiliary power generators turned on, restoring power to vital points. All the personnel on duty, after a moment of general panic, moved to understand what was happening.

Liam, with the confidence of someone who knew what to do, crossed the entrance to the gardens on Via

Montebello. Luca followed him at a distance, pretending to consult a tablet with electrical diagrams.

They were about to reach the service door when the sound of footsteps made them stop. A group of security personnel discussing the ongoing blackout turned the corner. One of them noticed Luca dressed as a maintenance technician and said, "Hey, you!" he called to him in an authoritative tone. "What happened to the electrical system?".

Luca, with his heart pounding but his voice firm, replied: "That's why I'm here. We've detected anomalies in the control system, there could be unexpected power surges."

The guards looked at him for a moment, and then one of them waved him through. In the meantime, taking advantage of the moment of inattention, Liam had slipped unnoticed through the service door and, with a determined manner had immediately headed towards the stairs to reach the guesthouse on the first floor.

The first obstacle had been overcome.

The guesthouse occupied the wing of the embassy and was reserved for personnel from abroad in the event of a temporary stay in Rome. On some occasions, this wing was also used by MI6 to "hold" guests, and the professor, in this capacity, had been housed in a room.

Liam walked up the steps in silence. When he reached the hallway, the door to a room suddenly opened. A cleaning lady came out of the room with a trolley loaded with sheets and cleaning products. She looked at him for a moment, surprised as well, then gave him a quick greeting and continued on her way.

Meanwhile, Luca had reached the main control room. "I need access to the electrical panel," he told the security personnel who had arrived to check on the situation. While he was fiddling with the controls, he inserted his USB key into a hidden port.

Upstairs, Liam reached the professor's room. He knocked, and the professor opened. Liam motioned for him to be quiet, put on a maintenance suit, and told him to follow him.

He nodded, visibly surprised, but just as he was putting on the suit, a voice rang out from the corridor: "Special control on the first floor, a cleaning lady has reported suspicious movements."

Liam and the professor froze.

Door after door, the control advanced, and the sound of footsteps grew closer and closer. They were trapped.

It was at that moment that the embassy's security systems went crazy. All the doors unlocked with a loud click. The lights began to flash randomly. The security radios crackled with strong interference.

"What's going on?" The voice in the corridor was now alarmed. The footsteps moved towards the control room.

Liam smiled. Luca had managed to insert his USB key and had activated a program that interfered with the central control system, generating orchestrated chaos.

Taking advantage of the confusion, Liam and the professor moved, went down the stairs, and reached the side exit. At the door, Luca was waiting for them. After finishing his task and tampering with the system, he hid near the exit, waiting for the final escape.

Outside, Marco was ready at the wheel of a car. With measured steps, without running to avoid attracting attention, the professor and Luca approached the vehicle. Marco opened the back door, quickly glancing in both directions, and said: "Quick, inside! Quick!".

The professor curled up in the back seat, covered with some work tools, followed by Luca. "We made it," Marco muttered, immediately putting the car in first gear and starting to head for safety.

Liam, who had stayed behind to cover the escape, calmly returned to the embassy. He took off his overalls, threw it in a basket, and joined the other men of the staff who were trying to restore calm.

"What happened?" Liam asked two technicians who were arguing.

"It seems that there was an overload in the main electrical system, and the control computer went crazy. We're checking," replied the more robust of the two.

The whole action lasted less than 30 minutes.

9:20am | Villa Borghese

*O*n this sunny and relaxing day, Delaware was running in the gardens of Villa Borghese, enjoying the mild climate and the tranquility of the park. The sound of his rhythmic steps on the gravel path was the only noise in the morning silence.

Suddenly his phone vibrated.

He looked up for a moment in impatience for the interruption of that moment, then he took the device out of his pocket and read the message. "Technical blackout at the embassy's electrical system."

"What the hell is going on?" he muttered to himself, while his gaze hardened. It took him less than a second to realize that something was wrong, a breakdown due to overload on a Sunday was an impossible event. He turned, ran to some taxis parked inside the park, and got into the first one.

"To the British Embassy and hurry." Then he took out his phone and tried to call the security personnel, but the lines were all busy.

"Damn," he cursed, "this isn't a technical glitch, how can they not see that!"

10:00am | British Embassy

Upon reaching the embassy, he took out his identification badge, entered and ran towards the stairs to reach the guesthouse.

His heart, even though trained, was pounding with adrenaline and the anger that was building inside him.

When he reached the professor's room, he kicked open the door and found it empty. "Damn! I knew it!" he cursed.

A voice behind him made him turn around. It was Liam. "Delaware, what's going on? Where's the professor?" he asked in a neutral voice.

Delaware, smiling with a mix of frustration and irony, replied: "Just think, our professor ran away... But don't worry. This morning, before I left the embassy, I put a GPS tracker in his bag."

Liam tried to hide his surprise; he hadn't expected this move, and he realized that this beacon would compromise the safety of the professor and the kids. He had to think of a way to divert his attention.

"Well, give me a minute," Delaware continued, connecting the tracking system to his laptop. After a few moments, a map with a flashing signal appeared on the computer screen.

"It looks like it's heading towards the Lungotevere. Where are you going, my dear professor?" However, before he could finish, the GPS signal was interrupted.

"Damn! Damn, Liam. Someone was smarter than us. The beacon has been deactivated!".

Delaware cursed again under his breath and then left the room without even saying goodbye, while Liam breathed a sigh of relief. For the moment, the danger was over, but he knew that Delaware wouldn't stop until he found the professor and the kids.

The only way to stop him was to convince the director that there was still an open negotiation and that they should try to go down that road.

Liam took the report of what James had discovered, attached it to an email, and addressed it to the director, then picked up the phone and called him. "Good morning, director, I'm calling you on Sunday because the matter is very sensitive...".

After the report was over, the director's reaction was immediate; the hypotheses formulated, if true, changed the scenario and transformed a possible commercial battle into one with potential military consequences.

He asked: "Who besides you knows what you sent me?".

"Delaware, the professor, and the four boys, Sir," Liam replied, leaving out the presence of the Monsignor during the interactions with James.

The director, realizing that the situation was getting complicated, said, "Liam, I will immediately make a call to the Prime Minister. In the meantime, do not move and inform Delaware not to move; we cannot take the wrong steps".

12:00pm | Via della Conciliazione

The Antico Caffè on Via della Conciliazione, with its spectacular view of St. Peter's Basilica, had been chosen as the meeting place. Inside, two figures linked by a common goal but separated by profound differences were about to meet.

Llorente, with his robe as black as the night and his collar as white as the purity he professed, sipped a bitter coffee with ice, thinking about the words he would have to say to justify the change of refuge.

In front of him, Liam, with his impeccable gray suit despite the rain, embodied the essence of the British intelligence service; with a sharp gaze he observed the surrounding environment, with the ease of someone who had seen a lot in his career and was no longer surprised by anything and it was he who broke the silence.

"Monsignor, it is a real pleasure to see you again," he said with a tone that anticipated his protest.

"The pleasure is mine," the Monsignor replied, with a Spanish accent, before extending his hand to Liam in a sign of peace. Then he added, in a soothing tone: "I imagine that you are very surprised and saddened by the change of shelter that I orchestrated, right?".

Liam could not deny it. His face made it clear that he did not appreciate the unexpected change of plan, which had saved the boys and the professor from certain interception by Delaware, but which remained, in any case, a unilateral decision not shared.

"I admit that your initiative surprised me," Liam replied, trying to overcome this moment of initial disagreement. "In any case, I would prefer to put aside the motivations and discuss the reasons that brought us to this situation."

Llorente nodded: "I agree."

Liam turned in an attempt to intercept a waiter and continued: "Before we go any further, allow me to express my gratitude for your presence at the coworking yesterday. For me, and I am sure also for Luca and the boys, it was a real surprise".

The Monsignor smiled with calm satisfaction.

"Sometimes, Liam, reality exceeds expectations. But let's get to the reason for this meeting. What is the proposal you wanted to advance?".

Liam, lowering his voice, replied: "My government has asked me to explore with you the possibility of extending the Serica agreement to the United Kingdom".

Then, leaning toward the Monsignor as if seeking a moment of greater attention, he added: "Alternatively, they have asked me to evaluate with you the possibility of negotiating a new bilateral agreement, with reference to common interests in Africa".

The Monsignor listened while keeping his gaze fixed on the interlocutor.

"Dear Liam, we will carefully evaluate your requests. Peace, prosperity, and the conciliation that this path is inspired by have always been at the heart of our efforts."

Liam, happy to hear words that in some way hinted at a possible opening, added: "What we discovered yesterday about China's real intentions radically changes the picture. Unfortunately, as you can imagine, the rules of the game are no longer the same."

It was clear to both of them that the position of openness towards China now had to be reevaluated in light of what was discovered.

Liam continued: "I would like to bring another sensitive issue to your attention. The four boys and the professor are still in serious danger. Having hidden them for the moment helps, but it certainly cannot be the definitive solution. I believe it is our precise duty to find a way out that puts them all in a position of safety.

The solution could be considered an integral part of the negotiation on this extension of the agreement." Llorente thought for a moment: "Your proposal is bold. Offering the future safety of the professor and the four boys in exchange for an extension of the existing agreement strikes a chord that we both love to play. But how does your government plan to handle the magnetic cover that the Chinese intend to implement?".

Liam answered confidently: "We have already begun to evaluate options. I anticipate that my government is also prepared to ensure that James remains in your hands, without any additional action on our part. I can assure you that my government and its allies will not back down from the challenges posed by this new technology, whatever they may be."

This implied the possibility of military action in Africa as a defense against this Chinese expansion and its magnetic cover.

With this last sentence Liam stood up, shook the Monsignor's hand and left the café, knowing that he had used the right words to convince him to support his cause. The only hope left was that wisdom, and diplomacy could guide everyone towards an agreement.

Monday 2:00pm | Vatican City

*I*n the early afternoon, the Monsignor once again crossed the courtyard of San Damaso to reach the Apostolic Palace. The sun high in the sky cast short shadows on the marble floor, while his footsteps echoed in the solemn silence of the Vatican.

As he walked, he considered how to present the British request to the Secretary of State, without it being perceived as an ultimatum.

"Good morning," the warm voice of His Eminence greeted him as soon as he crossed the threshold of the study. "Our meetings are becoming a habit, don't you think?", he added. The smile on his face was genuine, but his eyes betrayed a deep awareness of what was happening.

"Your Eminence, the pleasure of meeting you is such that these meetings do not feel like a burden," Llorente replied with a slight bow.

The Secretary of State approached until Llorente could hear his breathing: "Alberto, spare me the diplomacy. Your plan... that leak from Mexico, the professor's algorithms used as bait..."

He paused, scanning his face. "And then that death by poisoning, so... convincing. You brought the wolves out of the woods, just as you wanted."

Llorente didn't look away and kept smiling: "Your Eminence, you give me too much credit." Their eyes met in a silent duet, "I just... tickled their greed. Human nature is predictable when it comes to power." Both knew they were walking on the edge of a precipice, and a single misstep could bring everything down.

In the distance, the bells of St. Peter's began to ring, their tolling like an ominous omen that echoed through the walls of the Vatican.

"Dear Alberto," the Secretary said, moving toward a window, letting the light filter through the ancient glass and illuminate his face. "The Chinese are buying Africa with loans at ridiculously low rates, sweet as honey, deadly as poison."

His words sounded grave. "But there is something even darker than money. The reports from our African dioceses... are cries in the dark." his hands were placed on the marble windowsill, and his gaze was lost in observing the faithful in the square below.

"Our Christian communities are becoming increasingly isolated minorities. Meanwhile, as we speak, mosques are sprouting like mushrooms, financed by the Gulf countries. They are using petrodollars to expand their influence in Africa."

The Cardinal turned: "The Chinese see the same specter that we see: an Africa prey to radicalism. Those eight cities that we will build... each with a church at the center, will represent a new hope. Places where Christian communities can thrive protected by a strong partner like China."

"The Serica agreement," he added as he watched the sunlight reflect on the floor, "is a masterpiece of impossible balances."

He looked up at the Monsignor: "The world only sees the economic aspect; we are building a safety net for our faithful. Those churches... are not simple stone buildings. They are the foundations of something much bigger."

This was supposed to be a new narrative. An agreement that would seal one of those alliances that on paper seemed impossible: on one side, the Holy See, the spiritual heart of Catholicism; on the other,

China, a global superpower with a communist political system.

Llorente nodded, appreciating the clarity of that strategic vision. But the Cardinal continued in a more thoughtful tone: "Of course, we know that England, France, the United States, and other countries do not look favorably on this agreement. For them, this is just another chapter in Chinese expansion in Africa, dressed up differently. But that is not the case."

"We know that, in Paris, the French president is furious about yet another contract signed by the Chinese in Kenya. The French consider these contracts to be real attacks on their historical interests," continued the Secretary, pouring himself a glass of water. "The United States fears losing control over all strategic resources. Spy planes have been flying over Chinese shipyards for some time now, and some American warships have begun to patrol the African coasts more frequently."

"I understand, Your Eminence," said the Monsignor, "I believe that the situation in London is not so different. We are observing the English reaction these days. Their anger is seeping from every line of their newspapers."

The Secretary nodded. "Dangerous times, Alberto. Proceeding with caution is essential."

After this intense exchange, the Secretary stopped, looked at the Monsignor's face and said: "Serica was conceived as a détente agreement, as it places us by right in the position of mediator between individual interests, promoting dialogue, cooperation and working to ensure that the interests of all parties are respected".

Then, clasping his hands in prayer, he continued: "I am of a certain age, I do not deny that I am confident in the possibility of organizing an official visit of the Chinese Prime Minister to Rome during the next Holy Year. An unprecedented historical event, a reminder of the power that human beings have to overcome divisions and unite for the greater good. My last gift to the Church".

Suddenly, the Cardinal stopped, looked at the Monsignor again and, in a voice that seemed to be that of a father who notices something wrong in his son's eyes, said: "Alberto, what are you hiding from me?".

Llorente sighed slightly, his face betraying measured concern. "Your Eminence," he began, choosing his words carefully, "unfortunately, I have some unpleasant news. Our actions have triggered unexpected reactions from some intelligence services. The British...".

"The British only see the surface...", the Cardinal interrupted him, "they do not understand that we are playing a more complex game. If Africa were to fall under an all-encompassing Islamic influence, the consequences would be catastrophic not only for the Church, but for the entire West".

"Your Eminence, I understand the risk. However, it must be said that the British have been extremely incisive. They have activated all their channels to decipher what the Chinese were building", Llorente continued.

"Well, they will have discovered that they are building eight churches and that these will become part of eight new cities in Africa, right?".

"Yes, and in itself it wouldn't be a problem, but then they continued the research and, using the very AI technology that we know, they discovered that the Chinese military is supporting the project shared with us with another military project aimed at creating a magnetic umbrella over all of central Africa to keep the continent in check".

The Secretary put a hand to his mouth almost to stop his breathing, then seemed to catch his breath and without continuing the speech said: "In fifteen minutes, an ambassador from the British government will come to us. Contrary to what is required by protocol, I would ask you to stay. Your presence will be of great help to me. I believe that you, more than anyone else, have the duty to assist me in this delicate meeting".

"Certainly, Your Eminence", replied the Monsignor.

His Eminence returned to his desk, his hands clasped in prayer before him. "If the British decide to use this information to sabotage the Serica agreement, we could lose the entire continent of Africa. And with it, millions of faithful."

"The priority, Your Eminence, is to find a way to stop the Chinese military project without compromising the main agreement. The stakes are infinitely higher than the British can imagine," the Monsignor concluded.

Just then, an aide knocked on the door, interrupting the conversation. "Your Eminence, the two guests have arrived." The Cardinal and the Monsignor exchanged a final, knowing look.

The game was far from over.

3:00pm |
Vatican City

"**G**ood morning, Ambassador. I am very pleased to meet you and Mr. Smith. I apologize for not having given you advance notice, but Monsignor Llorente will be joining us," said the Secretary of State, inviting the two guests to sit on a sofa.

"Mr. Smith, I consider the Monsignor a mutual friend. I am sure that you both care deeply about the story that involves us. Tell me, how can I assist you?".

The British Ambassador spoke: "Your Eminence, our intelligence service has detected that a delegation from the Holy See has recently signed an agreement with the Chinese government. Now, my government does not intend to carry out any act of interference, but it considers it appropriate to explore the possibility of extending this agreement to the United Kingdom, given the economic and strategic importance at stake."

The Cardinal, with his hands clasped in front of him, after a moment of reflection, began to respond in a calm and serene voice: "I understand your concerns. However, I must remind you that agreements with other states are sensitive and confidential matters. We cannot unilaterally extend such agreements to other nations simply because of their request. The Holy See is always open to dialogue with everyone, if the British government wishes to discuss an agreement, we are willing to listen to the proposals, but we cannot extend or change agreements made with others".

The ambassador tried to hide his concern, but he understood the reasons of the other party well: "Your Eminence, I will pass on your message to my government. I would propose to organize a preliminary meeting and involve a diplomatic delegation to explore what possibilities there are. Do you think this can be done?"

The Cardinal smiled: "Certainly. I will have our office contact your embassy to work out a timetable that is convenient for both parties."

Then, in a slightly more serious tone, he added: "Before I take my leave, allow me to emphasize the crucial role that the International Court of Justice plays in ensuring respect for international law."

The ambassador seemed intrigued by the clarification, but he could not understand its connection to the ongoing discussion. "Certainly, the role of the ICJ is fundamental. Why do you remind me of this, Your Eminence?"

The Secretary, in an even more decisive tone: "As an elected judge of this Court, I can maintain that information obtained through assets owned by a state cannot be used to harm that state."

The Cardinal paused to allow the ambassador to fully understand his words and then continued: "The Holy Father has made it clear that the assets of the Holy See have a universal destination and that the institutions and entities that have acquired them act as trustees, not as private owners. These assets must be used in the name and under the authority of the Holy Father, for the pursuit of institutional purposes and for the common good".

Then, standing up and looking at the ambassador, he said:

"In this light, the artificial intelligence algorithms that we know are to be considered assets of the property of the Holy See, as is all the information that is gathered and collected through them. I am sure that your government cannot but agree with this indisputable certainty".

"I understand, Your Eminence. I will also convey this message to my government. We appreciate your transparency and your commitment to maintaining international peace and justice", nodded the ambassador who had well understood the meaning of these words.

The Secretary, to lighten the tense moment, placed his hand on Liam's shoulder while he was still sitting and calling him by his real name, said: "Dear Liam, before we say goodbye I must congratulate you on your daughter's graduation and give you a small gift on behalf of me and the entire Holy See".

Then, withdrawing his hand from his shoulder: "They tell me that you graduated in Engineering from the university dedicated to our Pedro Arrupe. I won't hide the fact that I was surprised to learn that you attend a Jesuit institution, but after all, who better than us can understand traditions? It does you credit to maintain this strong bond with Rhodesia, or rather with Zimbabwe.

Looking away, he added: "Peace be with you, dear Ambassador."

Finally, before escorting the two guests to the exit, without saying another word, he turned to Liam and smiled at him.

4:00pm | Vatican City

The Secretary, pleased and satisfied with the meeting that had just ended, turned to Monsignor Llorente: "Alberto, have you noticed? No mention of the thorniest issue, what you call magnetic umbrella. We know that the English are aware of the project. Not addressing it leads me to think that they want to leave the initiative to us. In other words, we must think about it before the situation degenerates".

Then, after a moment of reflection, he said again: "If that is the case, then we will have to find a way to solve this problem. The Chinese military has changed the cards on the table. We must make sure that these cards are blown without interrupting the real game. We cannot wait for others to do it for us".

The Cardinal was aware that if there was someone within those walls capable of finding a solution, that someone was right there, standing in front of him.

Llorente nodded, a gesture that indicated that he had fully understood the message His Eminence was conveying to him.

After a cordial greeting, Llorente walked towards the Vatican gardens, his hands clasped behind his back as he walked along the well-kept paths. The light wind caressed his face, and the sound of pebbles under his feet accompanied his thoughts.

To his left, he saw the kite fountain, with its sculptures and water features, and then the square garden, a perfect example of an Italian garden, with its geometric and symmetrical shapes, an ideal place to stop for a moment and reflect.

In the silence of that moment, his mind wandered among a thousand possibilities, desperately searching for a solution that could neutralize the threat of the Chinese military project while safeguarding the delicate balance of the Serica agreement. He could not allow years of diplomacy and progress to go up in smoke.

It was then, in that quiet, that a sudden intuition struck him like a bolt from the blue. A bold plan, perhaps reckless, but one that could work. A final, risky gamble that could change everything.

With renewed determination, he set off with determined steps toward the operations room, while in his mind, the details of the plan began to take shape.

4:00pm |
Porta Sant'Anna

$\mathcal{L}$ iam had made an enemy of Delaware and the entire ESOD organization, due to his favorable attitude to finding a negotiated solution and above all because he was suspected of having been the one to organize and direct the professor's escape.

After his hasty return to London, Delaware, going against all internal MI6 regulations and perhaps even common sense, had given the order to eliminate Liam. His murder was not to be silent, but on the contrary, it had to make a lot of noise. The order given to the hitman was to kill him right in front of the Vatican walls, after his meeting, in broad daylight.

It was not to be a simple murder but a strong signal, to be sent inside the walls, to convince the Holy See to sit down and find a joint solution to the Chinese question without raising too many demands.

The hitman, after receiving instructions and the order to act, had positioned himself on a terrace at the corner of Via di Porta Angelica and Borgo Vittorio, ready to strike with surgical precision.

Below him, the crowd of tourists walked by, unaware of the drama that was about to unfold. The hitman watched every movement through the rifle scope, keeping a controlled breath. Without emotion, he waited, going over every detail of the plan and considering all the variables: angle, light, temperature, wind.

And yet, under that armor of indifference, an imperceptible shiver ran down his spine. It wasn't fear. Today he was about to commit the murder of a fellow countryman and not an enemy, and what's more in front of Porta Sant'Anna, in front of the Vatican walls, among thousands of innocent tourists. This was a feeling he had never felt in his entire life.

Unaware of what was about to happen, Liam walked in the company of the ambassador toward the large exit door. His expression was relaxed and satisfied at having found a good initial compromise, even if the issue of the Chinese magnetic umbrella had remained pending and not discussed during the meeting.

Now ready to pull the trigger, the hitman saw a reflection, lasting a fraction of a second. It reminded him of Afghanistan: such a reflection meant an enemy sniper lying in wait, but here we were in the center of Rome and he only had the Apostolic Palace in front of him.

He didn't have time to think about anything else. A shot fired right from the Apostolic Palace less than four hundred meters away hit him squarely in the head, leaving him lifeless on the terrace. A silent, subsonic shot, fired by someone who had a lot of experience. The single bullet had hit him without leaving him any escape.

The barrel of a German-made Mauser, modified in Switzerland, retracted from a window of the building and the window closed.

5:00pm | Vatican City

Meanwhile, the Monsignor, having reached the heart of his control room, found Martini and the four boys waiting impatiently for him. He had removed them from general attention and diverted them to the Domus Sanctae Marthae, a residence located inside the Holy See.

This structure, used to host Cardinals during conclaves, could accommodate other guests on special occasions. The residence guaranteed greater security than any other place could have offered, including the refuge recommended by Liam.

Llorente turned to the boys decisively: "I have developed a strategy, but to implement it, we will need to take risks. In reality, we have to make one last bet".

"What is it about?", asked Marco, curious and worried.

"We need to involve the journalist Alessandro Conti. He could be the right person to help us solve this whole story".

Luca shook his head: "I have read about him. He is a very tenacious journalist, but why him? How can he help us stop Chinese military projects?"

"Exactly. You said it right; he has great tenacity. I had some research done on him," said the Monsignor, and explained that Moro, who was in charge of investigating the journalist, had discovered that Alessandro, during his period of study in Germany, had created excellent relationships with the most important NGOs.

Llorente knew that obtaining the support of these large organizations would be essential to spread the news of the magnetic shield globally and to put great pressure on the Chinese government. However, he was also aware that the Holy See could not afford to expose itself directly with this request. An intermediary was needed.

"Interesting," said Luca, "but how can we involve him without arousing suspicion about us?"

"We cannot contact him directly. We need an unsuspecting intermediary," said the Monsignor, "someone who can pass the information we have gathered to Conti without attracting attention."

The Monsignor took a piece of chalk and began to draw on the blackboard a diagram of the path that the information would have to follow to be credible and reach the public without compromising them.

"We could send them the documentation anonymously," Luca said, his eyes fixed on the blackboard.

The Monsignor shook his head. "No, it has to be done by someone who knows how to do it better than us and who knows how to protect us." He paused and then turned to Marco. "You told me you received messages from an anonymous source. Are you able to respond to that contact?".

"Of course, I can still use the channel, but we don't know who will read it," Marco replied.

The Monsignor drew a circle around Alessandro Conti's name written on the blackboard. "As I was saying, the time has come to take a risk."

Llorente's gamble was precisely to focus on this anonymous contact to pass the information to the journalist. The Monsignor hoped to find the person he expected to find. The right person.

"Marco, write this message," the Monsignor ordered.

"We are ready to spread what we know online, but we need your help to get some documentation to a contact of ours. You have to do this using your channels, shielding us."

Marco typed quickly and sent the message. A few seconds later, a short response appeared on the phone screen: "To whom?".

"Alessandro Conti of *L'Informazione*," Marco replied without hesitation. After this last message, the communication went silent again.

"Quick," the Monsignor said, "you have to configure James so that he begins a silent and widespread distribution action online of the information we have. He has to position it so that it is identifiable but does not allow us to understand who posted it and when. I don't think I need to tell you anything else; the objective is clear."

The atmosphere in the room became heated, and they were back to action.

The boys immediately got to work. The stakes were high, and every detail of the plan had to be executed to perfection.

10:20pm |
L'Informazione

That evening Alessandro had lingered in the newsroom. He was constantly adding elements to what he had already discovered: the lawyer's death, the professor, the boys, the Vatican services, but he still couldn't get a complete picture of what was happening.

His cell phone suddenly vibrated. It was a message from an unknown number: "Hotel Bernini, room 304, code 8202, there are documents for you on the desk." The text was concise and in English.

He looked at his watch: it was 10:20 p.m. He thought that the moment was perfect. The streets of Rome at that hour were still busy, and his entrance to the hotel would have been confused with that of the customers returning after dinner. He stood up, put on his jacket, and moved.

The night air of Rome hit him as soon as he left the building.

The streets, as expected, were still busy with tourists going out or looking for a restaurant. Everything around him seemed normal. He walked and didn't think he was in any danger, even though he had learned never to trust appearances completely.

As he walked toward the Hotel Bernini, he couldn't help but wonder if, after that night, he would finally be able to come to some conclusions.

The hotel loomed before him. Alessandro crossed the hall with a confident step as if he were a guest of the hotel. The girls at the reception barely glanced at him and greeted him without asking him anything.

He went up the stairs instead of taking the elevator, an old habit that had already saved his life once.

On the third floor, the corridor was immersed in an unreal silence. Room 304. He stopped for a moment in front of the door. He knocked three times. Silence. There was no answer. He typed in the code and the door opened.

Alessandro entered the room cautiously; the light of a small lamp had turned on when he opened the door. The room was modern, welcoming, and everything seemed in perfect order. On the desk, a briefcase and a copy of the London Times awaited his arrival. The brown leather briefcase seemed to almost glow in the lamplight; the Times was sitting on top, like a silent invitation.

He approached slowly. He picked up the paper. It was yesterday's edition, open to the economics page. One story was highlighted in yellow; it talked about Chinese investment in Africa, but it was just a piece of routine. The real message must be in the briefcase.

His fingers ran over the soft leather of the briefcase, finding the combination already set. A soft click and the contents were in his hands: a series of documents meticulously organized in numbered folders, a USB stick, and some satellite photographs.

The first photo showed what looked like a normal construction site, but the notes in the margins told a different story. GPS coordinates, dates, code names.

He quickly checked the time: it was 11:10 p.m.; he had been in the room too long already. He packed everything in the backpack he had brought and closed the briefcase, leaving it empty on the table.

Before leaving, he made sure the room was exactly as he had found it, except for those documents that now weighed like lead in his backpack.

The return through the corridor and the stairs was tense, every sound amplified by the silence of the night. In the hall, the girls at the reception barely looked up, a little surprised to see him come out again, but they said nothing.

Outside, Rome was still alive, the tourists walking around unaware provided him with perfect cover. He didn't go straight back to the newsroom; he took a longer route, changing direction several times, occasionally stopping to check the shop windows to make sure no one was following him.

Only when he was sure he was alone did he head towards the newspaper.

The building was deserted at that hour. He went up to his floor, locked the door to his office, and finally, with his heart still beating hard, opened his backpack.

Under the light of his lamp, the documents revealed their shocking content. Graphs, technical reports, private correspondence, all pointed to a project far larger and more disturbing than he had ever imagined. Satellite photographs showed a very extensive network of installations, but it was one document in particular that caught his attention.

It was an internal memory. The text was in English and Chinese, and it spoke of "continental-scale control of communications" and "ultimate technological supremacy."

His hands were shaking as he inserted the USB stick into his computer. The files were encrypted, but the password had been handwritten on the back of the last photograph. When the documents opened on the screen, Alessandro understood that what he had in his hands was a project with potentially devastating geopolitical implications, capable of altering the balance of power in the world.

He felt the weight of the discovery weigh on his shoulders. In twenty years of journalism, he had never encountered anything like it. With his fingers still shaking, he grabbed the phone: there was only one person who could help him fully understand the scope of what he had found.

He picked up the phone and dialed Bauer's number.

Doctor Michael Bauer, with his experience in geopolitics and military technology, was the only person he trusted and the only one with whom he could share a discovery of this magnitude.

"Michael, it's Alessandro," he whispered into the phone as soon as the call was accepted, casting a nervous glance around the empty newsroom.

Midnight |
Rome and Berlin

Alessandro was born in Bolzano. After graduating in Italy, he decided to follow his dream and enroll at the

Hochschule für Journalismus in Berlin to study journalism. Here, he began to build a network of relationships that led him to work with major NGOs. The most significant experience was with Save4Africa, an organization dedicated to sustainable development in large cross-border areas in Africa.

In those years, Alessandro had traveled to numerous African countries, documenting the struggles and aspirations of local communities. Those trips had not only enriched him humanly and professionally but had transformed his way of seeing the world.

It was precisely in that period that he established a close collaboration with the director of Save4Africa. Michael Bauer was a visionary, a man of great experience who Alessandro soon began to consider his teacher and mentor.

"Alessandro!" Bauer replied with an exclamation that showed great pleasure in receiving this call. Then, with his characteristic German accent: "It's always a pleasure to hear from you. To what do I owe this call at midnight?".

Alessandro wasted no time and got straight to the point, his voice tense with urgency: "Sorry. I have received documents that speak of an upcoming Chinese military installation in Central Africa. They want to build a sort of magnetic dome that could alter the geopolitical balance of the entire continent."

"I have read about these technologies," Bauer replied, "but I always thought they were still very remote. Do you have any concrete proof?".

"Yes Michael, unfortunately I have received documents and photographs that confirm China's intention to install a magnetic shield by the end of next year at the latest."

Alessandro's voice continued to grow in intensity: "I need your help and the full support of Save4Africa. We need to create very strong international pressure against this crazy military project."

A brief silence fell on the other end of the line. Bauer was clearly weighing the implications of what he had just heard. "Send me a copy of the material. I will distribute it through our network. What's your plan?"

Bauer was waiting for a response when he paused. "Wait… something is already happening online," he said, looking at his computer.

The first rumors were appearing on blogs in Asia. A reporter for HKNews had just published a story about the possible existence of Chinese military installations in Africa. Reuters had picked up the story, citing "well-informed anonymous sources."

It was clear that someone else was starting to spread information, but the source was unidentifiable.

"With your help," Alessandro replied, "I was thinking of organizing a conference call to invite the leaders of the main NGOs and make them aware of the material we have."

Alessandro's voice became more forceful as he laid out his strategy: "We need to join forces and launch a global campaign to raise awareness and put pressure on the Chinese government."

"I'll contact our partners tomorrow morning," Bauer replied, "but you have to be careful. There are huge interests behind this project. They won't just stand by and watch while you try to stop them."

Alessandro was clutching the phone. "I know, but we can't let them go ahead. This project must be stopped at all costs."

"Okay. But be careful," Bauer concluded before hanging up the call.

In Berlin, in his office lit only by the light of streetlamps filtering through the large windows, Bauer remained still, staring at a large map of Africa hanging on the wall.

The evidence he had just received on his computer was more explosive than he had imagined. His mind was already racing to the possible consequences of what was about to be unleashed.

He rose from his worn leather chair and approached the window of his tenth-floor office. Nighttime Berlin stretched out below him like a sea of lights. The Fernsehturm, with its sphere, stood out illuminated against the dark sky, while beyond it, the lights of the Brandenburg Gate shone like a beacon in the night. Just as thirty years earlier, when the Wall fell, Berlin was unknowingly preparing to be the center of another crucial moment in history.

Michael took his phone out of his pocket; he thought it was already 7:00am in Hong Kong, and he dialed the number of Emily Chen, director of Green Earth Asia.

"Emily, we have a very critical situation. I am sending you some very confidential documents. Read them immediately and call me back as soon as you can." The director understood the urgency: "I will read them immediately and call you back."

As soon as the call ended, Bauer sent an urgent message to the representatives of the other eleven major international NGOs, calling a conference call for the following morning.

Tuesday 7:30am | Berlin

It was 7:30 in the morning. The light of the Berlin dawn filtered through the curtains of the office when Bauer placed the emergency call.

In a few minutes, his computer screen gradually filled with worried faces, connected from every corner of the planet. Emily Chen, already informed during the night, appeared wide awake from her office in Hong Kong, where it was already late afternoon. Sarah McKenzie connected visibly sleepy from the American West Coast, where it was still late at night. Finally, Alessandro connected from Rome.

It was unusual to receive a conference call with such short notice, so everyone assumed the worst.

"Gentlemen," Bauer began, his voice firm despite the gravity of the situation, "what I am about to show you will change your understanding of China's projects in Africa."

The images began to scroll across the screens and the silence became heavy. The faces of the participants grew darker and darker as the details of the project revealed themselves before their eyes.

"My God," Sarah McKenzie of Human Rights said, clapping her hand to her mouth, "they're building a continent-wide system of control."

"Not only that," Emily Chen said, her pale face illuminated only by the light from her screen, "I've compared this data to our field readings. We've been seeing magnetic anomalies for the past six months, but we thought they were natural disturbances…" Her voice cracked slightly. "Now it's clear they were already testing the system."

Juan Morales of Aid Without Borders shook his head, frustration evident on his face. "But how can we fight back? The Chinese government will deny it."

"Not if we all act together!" Bauer said, banging his fist on the desk. "United, they won't stop us."

He leaned toward the webcam, his eyes shining with determination.

In the weeks
that followed...

*I*n the weeks that followed, a perfect storm hit the Chinese project, orchestrated with precision by Alessandro Conti and Dr. Bauer.

Green Earth Asia kicked off the show with a technical report that sent shockwaves through the scientific world. Emily Chen, her eyes darkened from sleepless nights analyzing data, presented irrefutable evidence of magnetic anomalies.

Sarah McKenzie of Human Rights appeared before the UN Security Council with a briefcase full of classified documents. Her voice didn't waver as she described a dystopian future in which an entire continent's communications would be at the mercy of a single government.

"What you see here," she said, pointing to a map projected on the wall, "is not progress. It's control. It's not help. It's domination."

The Chinese government attempted to deny the accusations, but each denial was quickly drowned out by new evidence.

On social media, the battle went viral. #AfricaIsNotYourLab spread like a digital wildfire, fueled by the passion of millions of young activists. Videos, testimonies, technical analyses: each post was a new nail in the project's coffin.

The turning point came when Emily Chen flew to Europe to testify before the European Parliament. She presented a dossier that silenced the assembly in Brussels.

"What we have discovered," Emily declared, "is beyond imagination. It is not just technology. It is an attempt to rewrite the future of a continent."

In the wake of this hearing, the World Bank and the IMF began to reconsider their loans to China. The message was clear: "Money must follow morality," or at least that was the rule this time.

The Chinese government found itself completely isolated. The evidence was too strong to deny, the public pressure too strong to ignore. The press conference in Beijing was brief and controlled. The Foreign Ministry spokesman, with an impassive mask on his face, announced that the Government of the People's Republic of China had decided to take a "reassessment pause" for the magnetic umbrella project.

The promise to continue all other development projects underway in Africa, including new cities, was reiterated without exception, even allowing for external supervision.

In his office in Berlin, illuminated by the setting sun, Bauer received the call he had been waiting for.

"We did it," Alessandro said, his voice still incredulous.

"Yes," Bauer replied, looking at the photographs on his desk, reminders of thirty years of fighting for justice. "But it wasn't just our merit. It was the demonstration that when the truth comes to light, not even the most powerful country can hide it."

Alessandro approached the window of his apartment in Rome. In the square, a group of young people was playing soccer. "You know something, Michael?" he said into the phone, "Looking at these kids, I understand that the future of these technologies will be in their hands alone." Bauer smiled.

Holy See – Rome

*I*n the quiet of a small private chapel, the boys, the professor, and the Monsignor gathered, not to celebrate but to reflect on what had happened. The soft light of the candles danced on the frescoed walls and created an intimate and solemn atmosphere.

The Monsignor, after a long moment of meditation, turned towards them with a serene but intense expression. His voice resounded calm and deep: "In this story, I clearly see the hand of Providence. It was not only a victory of human ingenuity but a powerful reminder of our role as guardians of the truth. As Saint Augustine said: *The truth is like a lion, you do not need to defend it; leave it free, and it will defend itself*".

His words echoed in the chapel, penetrating the hearts of all present. Each of them felt the weight and honor of the path they had undertaken and the responsibility that came with it.

Suddenly, Luca's phone vibrated, breaking the silence. Hesitantly, he pulled out the device and read the message that appeared on the screen. It was from their mysterious ally: "You did very well. Congratulations."

A thin smile played across his lips as he passed the phone to the others, allowing them to read the message. No one said a word. The silence that followed was filled with gratitude and awareness as the sun continued its descent behind the dome of St. Peter's, painting the Roman sky with the colors of eternity.

Sussex – South of England

*D*elaware was on his way to Steyning, Sussex. Like every weekend, he had left London City Airport on a private jet and landed at Brighton Airport after just thirty minutes. A short flight that this time had seemed interminable.

Arriving in Brighton, he had climbed into his armored Jaguar, driven by a trusty chauffeur who would take him to his estate in half an hour. During the journey, he had been drumming his fingers nervously on his Italian leather briefcase.

The news from Rome was tormenting him: his hitman found dead near the Vatican, Liam still alive, the Italian secret services starting to connect the dots. Too many variables and too much risk. Sweat was beading on his forehead despite the air conditioning on full blast.

A few miles away, on a hill overlooking Steyning, a green Land Rover with the typical yellow license plates moved silently along a dirt road, kicking up a thin trail of dust in the humid Sussex air. The vehicle climbed confidently up the hill, guided by expert hands that betrayed years of experience on terrain far more hostile than this.

The driver, a man with a face carved from granite, studied the landscape through the windshield, his blue eyes observing every detail like precision sensors.

The Land Rover stopped at a precise point, calculated to the millimeter. On the roof, what to a casual observer might have looked like a normal camping platform, in reality hid a perfectly designed shooting platform.

The man pulled a McMillan TAC-50 from his military bag with the reverence of a priest handling a sacred chalice. Every movement was fluid, precise, the result of years of training and missions.

He mounted the telescope with measured gestures, his breathing slowing as he entered that state of absolute concentration that only snipers know. Through the precision optics, the Victoria pastry shop appeared clear despite the 800 meters (about half mile) of distance.

Eight hundred meters seems like a lot but that distance in reality to him was almost nothing; over the years, some English and Canadian snipers with a McMillan TAC-50 had managed to hit targets placed at much greater distances.

The ritual of Delaware Friday was his doom. The Victoria Cake Shop, those damned sweets his wife loved so much, were the only weakness in an otherwise methodical and armored life.

At MI6, they taught you to avoid repetitive behavior, fixed routes, and predictable habits, in other words, not to make yourself easy to spot.

Delaware always followed these rules, never flew at a specific time, and always decided at the last minute which route to take between Brighton and Steyning. But there was one exception: the Victoria Cake Shop and its sweets. The man on the hill knew it and waited, motionless like a patient predator.

When the armored Jaguar stopped in front of the cake shop, time seemed to freeze. The driver got out, and the shop bell jingled. Delaware, alone in the cabin he thought impregnable, opened the Financial Times.

The shooter breathed in and began to whisper a melody: "À Courgenay, à Courgenay...".

The world was reduced to the reticle of the scope, to the physics of the bullet, to the mathematics of death. The bullet left the barrel at a speed of 2,700 feet per second.

One shot, a single shot. The bullet, the size of a finger, came with great force, shattering the armored glass designed to resist ordinary bullets, and hit Delaware squarely in the head.

The impact was violent. The Jaguar jerked like a wounded animal, rising on its side to immediately return to its four tires. The target had been hit with no escape. Delaware, thrown against the opposite seat, had fallen back into a pool of blood.

As the driver ran toward the car, the rifle had already been disassembled and placed in the bag with the same precision with which it had been assembled. The still-warm cartridge case slid into a dedicated pocket, no trace, no mistake.

The man crossed himself with the same hand that had just dealt death, touching his forehead, chest, and shoulders. The satellite phone vibrated with an incoming call.

"Good morning. Are you okay?"

The voice on the other end was calm, almost paternal.

"Yes," the shooter replied, his voice emotionless. "My hunger for justice has been satiated, Sir. I'll be back in four hours."

The Land Rover sped away down the dirt road, leaving behind only dust and the chaos unfolding around the Victoria Bakery.

Spring 2025

*T*he Monsignor crossed Bernini's colonnade as the first light of dawn painted the Roman sky pink. He headed toward his small private chapel, where every morning he found the meditation necessary to face the challenges that his role entailed.

That morning, however, he was not there just to pray.

On the small marble altar, next to the missal, lay a sealed envelope, delivered by trusted hands.

The paper, pure white, bore a sealing wax seal that broke with a slight crackle when the Monsignor opened it.

He pulled out a sheet of paper with a few lines of text, essential and precise:

"The Serica agreement is proceeding according to plan, and the eight churches have been completed. The professor has been hired by

Cambridge University, where he continues his work under British protection. The boys have returned to their lives, aware of having helped rewrite the future, while I, James, help a young writer write the plot of his first novel".

The Monsignor folded the sheet carefully, almost reverently, then put it in his pocket.

Meanwhile, an Air China Boeing 747-8I was cutting through the air, approaching Fiumicino.

On board, the General Secretary of the Chinese Communist Party, impeccable in his dark suit, was absentmindedly leafing through a dossier. Despite his impassive face, his mind was working feverishly, preparing every detail of the imminent meeting with the Holy Father.

In the cockpit, Commander Zhang, with years of experience behind him, asked for permission to land. His calm and professional voice hid the invisible concern of someone who was aware of the enormous responsibility that came with transporting one of the most powerful men on the planet.

"À Courgenay, à Courgenay
Il y a une fille qui fait parler d'elle
À Courgenay, à Courgenay
Il y a une fille qui fait parler d'elle
C'est la petite Gilberte
Qui sert à boire aux militaires
Elle est gentille, elle est mignonne La
petite fille de Courgenay"

Acknowledgements

A deep and heartfelt thanks go to Walter Ruffinoni, Andrea Colangelo, and Matteo Betto, who, with their sensitivity and expertise, have contributed significantly to the revision of the first draft, donating precious time and enlightening suggestions.

I would like to express my sincere gratitude to Daniela Pizzuti, Luca Iacomussi, and Giammarco Zorloni for their meticulous rereading of the second draft. Their attention to detail and their timely comments have allowed us to refine the text.

A special thanks goes to Nora De Giacomo, whose experience in editing and whose precious advice have accompanied this project for months, contributing significantly to its maturation and development.

My gratitude also goes to Michele Mangafà and Andrea Colangelo of Symphonie Partner, whose technical skills and willingness to discuss have guaranteed the accuracy and credibility of the more specialized aspects of the story.

Finally, the most intimate and profound thanks go to my wife, a constant presence and inexhaustible source of encouragement, who believed in this project from the beginning, encouraging me to cultivate this passion with dedication and perseverance.

Giuliano Zorloni

orn in Lombardy, engineer and entrepreneur, he divides his life between his home in Rome's Monti district and the international contexts of management consulting. Founder and Co-CEO of Symphonie Partners, as a free thinker he has published two acclaimed essays on non-hierarchical organizational models that earned him a professorship at the Faculty of Psychology at UER - European University of Rome. Vatican Veil (Velo Vaticano), his first novel, offers readers a story that combines his knowledge of the business world and international experience with the most innovative frontiers of artificial intelligence. Mentor to young entrepreneurs, he dedicates his free time to developing innovative projects, cultivating his passion for entrepreneurship and lean organization, conscious that "impossible" is a word to be used with great caution.